Slater Orchard

Slater Orchard

an etymology

Darcie Dennigan

FC2

TUSCALOOSA

FC2 is an imprint of The University of Alabama Press
Inquiries about reproducing material from this work should be addressed
to The University of Alabama Press

Book Design: Publications Unit, Department of English, Illinois State
    University; Director: Steve Halle, Production Intern: Morgan Folgers
Cover Design: Lou Robinson
Cover image: *Pear Tree* by Carl J. Dimitri; courtesy of the artist
Typeface: Baskerville

The author would like to thank the Rhode Island State Council of the
Arts for support provided during the creation of this work.

Library of Congress Cataloging-in-Publication Data

Names: Dennigan, Darcie, author.
Title: Slater orchard (an etymology) / Darcie Dennigan.
Description: Tuscaloosa, Alabama : The University of Alabama Press,
[2019] |
  Identifiers: LCCN 2019005728 (print) | LCCN 2019008261 (ebook) |
ISBN
  9781573668835 (E-Book) | ISBN 9781573660723 (paperback)
Classification: LCC PS3604.E5859 (ebook) | LCC PS3604.E5859 S58
2019 (print)
  | DDC 813/.6—dc23
LC record available at https://lccn.loc.gov/2019005728

for Marie Redonnet
and Brigit Pegeen Kelly

"the comedy stops itself but who can put an end to the laughter"

Slater Orchard

I AM NOT SURE IF SLATER ORCHARD IS REALLY AN ORCHARD. The word orchard is in my mouth. I want to look it up and see what it means. Where is the word orchard from. Orch. Char. My thinking isn't bringing me anyplace. Where is the word orchard from. I have already burnt the blue dictionary. I am not sure if Slater Orchard is really an orchard. No one calls it Slater Orchard but me.

Now that it is in my mouth, orchard is such a strange word. I can't say it right anymore. I'm saying orch-charred. But *Slater* is from the mills. This whole area used to be mills. It still is, though the mills don't make anything anymore. Slater Mill was the first mill, and the biggest. Slater was the man whose mill it was. He picked the best place on the river. Where it bends. There used to be a song about riverbends. Riverbend is a lonely word. But the mills were crowded. And noisy. Slater is from the biggest mill, which is quiet now. But still crowded. All the mills are quiet now and the river too. The mills killed it and its bend. The mills make nothing now but I am trying to make an orchard. Pear trees. Pear because the word sounds good to me. Also pear trees grow well in this area. I am trying to grow an orchard here. It is a new plan. The mills have all been split into parts. Partitions made the big workrooms into smaller rooms. Apartments. In an apartment is where I am. Where I have been with my new plan for an orchard. Which sounds lush. But it is an orchard of pears, which are not lush. Pears are clean, stripped-down fruit. They are an autumn fruit. Though fruit feels like too big a word for pears. Pear is an autumn thought.

My sister said, when the 1st baby died, what a shame it was that the parents had to pay for a burial. Burials are expensive. No one has planned for a baby's burial. Money is dear. The mills are quiet now, and the river is quiet. Babies are dear too. It is a shame that parents have to pay for a burial. No one with a baby has planned for its burial. The parents of the 1st baby to die had to pay. Though money is dear and the baby was very dear. There really is no ground in this area. There is just stone and cement. The mills go on for miles. There is very little ground and burial takes some planning. The way we say burial around here sounds like berry-all. Like a jubilee for raspberries. Though the way we say raspberry brings us back to death. Rasp berry. Even in the babies that have been born alive, born alive but going to die, there is no cry, my sister says. There is no cry but there is a rasp. My sister is more natural than I. Her plan is to keep the babies from dying. My plan is not that. Burying the babies is my plan. Burying them for free. My sister is more natural than I. I am thinking of money. I am thinking of money and mills and how there is very little ground for burial. There is very little ground here. But I am making an orchard. My sister is thinking of the water here. She says everyone knows that the river water is poison. Slater Mill was the first mill, and the biggest. My sister and I think Slater made denim. We think he must have. We have found denim cloth stacked in odd areas. And everyone talks about how the rocks around the riverbend are tinged blue. River-bend is a lonely word. Something in the river must turn the rocks blue. I agree that the river water is poisoned. Though we drink from the well and not from the river. When I say this to my sister, she smiles at me. My sister's plan is to keep the babies from dying. I do not smile at her when she is planning. She is more natural than I. It is natural for babies to live. My sister plans to do something about the water here. Which is blue. When I say that sounds like the water is sad, my sister smiles again. She is the younger sister. The mill rooms were partitioned into smaller rooms. And the smaller rooms leased as apartments. And the water all of us drink is from the well. We do not drink from the river. Everyone knows it is poisoned. Though blue is the word people use for the color of water, it is also the color of a dye. My sister and I think Slater milled denim here. I do not say to my sister how easy a step it is from dye to die. It is true that babies are dying. Though we drink from the well, there is seepage. My sister says there is seepage. And she smiles. It is a sad smile. My sister is the younger sister. She could still have babies. Her torso is long and fluid. River-bend is a lonely word. She could still have babies. But. Pear is an autumn thought. Autumn colors are burnt colors. Charred green and brown. Blue has no place in an autumn feeling. It is not natural that blue should mean death.

My sister's plan is to keep the babies from dying. She is going to clean the well. My plan is to bury babies for free. If any more die. I am trying to make an orchard here. Slater Orchard. Our plans are not altogether different. She is cleaning the water and I am cleaning the ground. We are both hiding our plans from the landlord. And I am also hiding my plans from my sister. There is seepage, my sister says. The poison river seeps into our well. This is what she thinks. It is true that the river is blue, maybe an unnatural blue, and it is true that the first baby to die was blue, blue-faced. I heard the landlord talking in his apartment while I was cleaning it. The baby was blue-faced, the landlord was saying. The baby was blue in the face and died. The landlord said, to the phone, the blue meant air was the problem. I told my sister this and she said the air is not his. The air is not his and so air cannot be his fault. So of course he will say air made the baby blue-faced. But, my sister says, it is the water. A cistern, she says, is the answer. The well must be too dirty. Even my sister, who cleans all day, could not clean the well. There is seepage. My sister has turned to a cistern. I smile at her. She thinks it is like a laugh and my sister turns away. That was a Monday. Mondays I clean the landlord's apartment. I clean all the apartments on the top floor of Slater Mill on Mondays. The top floor apartments are easiest to breathe in. My sister and I clean together. She dusts, I vacuum. I empty all the trash bins into the dumpster. She washes the floor with poison and water. My sister thinks about water. I think about trash. I like emptying the vacuum filter into the dumpster. Mondays are the days I clean the top floor. The landlord's apartment is the biggest. My sister and I clean together.

Tuesdays are for apartments on the middle floor

Wednesdays, ground floor

Thursdays, linens

Fridays, stairwells and hallways

Saturdays, windows

Sundays, I am making an orchard

Sundays I am making the orchard. Mondays I clean the landlord's apartment. Do it yourself this Monday, my sister says.
She wants to go to the roof. She is making a cistern. There is
seepage she says. Poison river means a poison well. The 1st
baby has died, and the 2nd. The water is to blame. The landlord says it is the air. I heard him on the phone. He said it was
a shame but he did not pay for the funeral. Though he knows
money is dear. He knows how high his rents are. Do it yourself, my sister says. I vacuum. I vacuum extra long so that my
sister can work on her cistern. Mondays are the days for my
sister and her cistern. Sundays I am making an orchard. My
sister has help from the maintenance man. Her cistern will be
on the roof. Her plan is progressing. The maintenance man
helps her. I do her part of the cleaning and I vacuum extra
long. The birds on the roof watch her. No one has seen me
making Slater Orchard. No one calls it Slater Orchard but me.
I chose the dumpster area. It is without birds. It is large and
fenced in. Its fence is high but the sun hits its ground for many
hours a day. Though the ground is still cement. And cement
is killed ground. I have already burnt the blue dictionary but
I will not forget the word cement. There is really very little
ground here. It is all cement. I will not forget when I looked up
cement. It's funny about words, how we say look up and not
look down. What is true is underneath. Burials. Berry-alls. Cement is to slay. I will not forget that. There is very little ground
here. Slater was the man who built this mill. It was the 1st and
the biggest. It killed the ground. I want to change the sign on

the entrance to the mill. To put a Y between the A and the T. Slayter Mill. Though no one would get the joke. Or if the tenants did get the joke, that would mean it was no longer a joke.

Last night I dreamt of Slater Orchard. There were 16 trees
in the fenced-in dumpster area. I did not see the dumpsters.
I did not see the incinerator. They must have grown smaller.
I did not care about them. There were 16 pear trees! It really
was Slater Orchard. 16 is not very many trees for an orchard.
It is a bare orchard. I knew then that I had been right to grow
pears. They are an autumn thought. Stripped down. And then
I thought struck down. Cement. Slay. But my pears had grown.
They had grown. I picked one and bit into it. The texture was
not good. The texture was not good but that did not worry
me. Pears are an autumn thought. You must strip them from
the trees and hide them away. Then the ground and sky are
stripped of color. When the ground and sky are white, the pear
is ripe. I picked one and bit into it. The texture was not good.
That did not worry me. I moved the pear away from my mouth
and saw its flesh. Its flesh was not white. The flesh was blue.
It was a horror. I thought, in the dream, this is not a dream.
I thought, it is a nightmare. And it was a nightmare. Even so,
when I woke from my dream of Slater Orchard, which was
a nightmare, I still needed to make the orchard. I thought of
how mare could be a horse. Mare could be a horse but there
is no ground for horses here. The mills go on for miles. Mare
could also be a sea and that is a possibility. I have never traveled
to the end of this river. It must meet a sea. The landlord has
a boat that he motors down the river. But I have never heard
him speak of a sea. I woke from my dream of Slater Orchard,
which was a nightmare. I thought of what mare could be. Not

a horse or a sea but a third meaning. I thought of the blue dye. Of the 1st baby dying. And the 2nd. Mare is also demoness of the corpses. It is a funny phrase. Demoness of the corpses is the third meaning. The truth is always buried in the word. When I woke I did not say the word nightmare to my sister. It was Sunday.

I have given the orchard ground a lot of thought. At first, to break the cement was what seemed to me the natural thing to do. I would break the cement and unbury the ground. I even thought that the ground underneath the cement might be rich. It had not grown things in such a long time. It had taken such a long break from growing things. Maybe the ground was rich and ready. But when my hammer broke past the last layer of cement, there was just dead ground. I am very strong from the cleaning. Stronger than my sister, who dusts. She dusts while I lift bins and empty them into the dumpster. It did not take me long, with the maintenance man's hammer, to break through the cement layers. Doesn't it seem the natural thing to do though, to break the cement and unbury the ground. But the ground was dead. It was not a natural dead. It was wet and smelled like blood. At first I thought it was blood. I thought that someone else had made a plan like mine. Someone else had buried bodies. A free funeral is not a new idea. Babies dying is nothing new. There was blood beneath the cement. This plan to bury babies was nothing new. My plan was not new. Underneath the concrete the ground was wet and smelled like blood. Except it was not red. The ground was blue. Dead and blue. Like the river. Cover it quickly. Cover it quickly and don't let the ground touch your skin. I covered it quickly with broken pieces of cement. Later I asked my sister if blood is ever blue. She smiled at me. She likes this kind of question. She smiled at me and her long fluid torso bent over. This is how she laughs. She can be very joyful. She likes to laugh. She is younger and more natural than I and she could still have babies. Though the babies here are dying. If blood is ever blue is something we don't know, my sister said. She said we don't know what our own blood is when it is buried in our skin. I wanted to tell her then of my plan. I am making an orchard! I wanted to tell her what is true is underneath. But I did not tell her. My sister says living things want to live. My sister is building a cistern to collect clean water. Living things want to live. But dead things want to live too. That is what I say. And that is the difference between me and my sister.

The landlord is wondering where my sister is. On Thursdays, it is linens. We wash all the landlord's towels and sheets. And his clothes. And we wash the rags we use to clean the building all week. And the mopheads. And our aprons. And we wash the flag that the landlord flies at the mill entrance. It is a white flag with a picture of the mill. It says Now Leasing. The landlord is always leasing. Some people don't stay long in this mill. They say there is a strange smell coming out of the floorboards. Or they say the river is poisoned. Cement is different to me now. It is keeping what is unnatural away. The river has seeped into the ground. It was the river that killed the ground. Now that I have seen what is beneath the cement, I think the cement is saving us. People don't want to see a poisoned river from their windows. Some people don't stay long. But where can they go. There are mills for miles.

The landlord is wondering where my sister is. Thursdays are linens. There is a laundry room on the ground floor of the mill. There is no basement. There is no basement, and this has always worried me. My sister and I do the linens on Thursdays. It takes all day. We also do a load of the clothes that we wear. We are supposed to do the landlord's towels and sheets and his clothes. And all the area rugs. Tenants are not allowed to use the laundry room. We also think it is okay to wash the rags and the mopheads. And the landlord specifically asks that we wash the Now Leasing flag. People don't stay too long. Tenants are forbidden to use the laundry room. My sister and I do. We do a load of the clothes that we wear each week. We do not think we are supposed to. The landlord, after all, is a landlord. The land part of his title is funny to me. There is no land here. There is no ground. What he is lord of is partitioned rooms, and the hallways, and the stairwells, and the dumpster area, and the Now Leasing flag. But the lord part is not funny. Lord might mean husband. My sister and I work for the landlord but we do not sleep with him. Lord might mean guardian of the loaves. This is why my sister and I think we are not supposed to wash our own clothes. Thursday is linens. The linens are the landlord's. It is his machine, his electricity, his water. His loaves. He is guarding them. It is just a small bite of his loaf that we are taking when we wash our clothes. It is a small load. That is what my sister says. She says, ours is a small load. It is just a small bite of his loaf we are taking. Guardian of the loaves would not appreciate my sister's logic. She does not care. My sister is younger than I. She is the unafraid one. I know what landlord means. Though the land part of his title is funny to me. It is funny to me, and it helps me to appreciate my sister's logic. She does not care. I know what landlord means and I try to care less. And now the landlord is wondering where my sister is. A 3rd baby has died. My sister and I are both speeding up our plans. Thursday is linens but my sister asked me to do them myself. She wants to be on the roof working on her cistern. The water is killing the babies. That's what my sister thinks. I don't know what materials she is using for the cistern. The maintenance man must have given her some. Thursdays while I clean the Now Leasing flag, my sister delivers the clean linens to the landlord's apartment. Today I am doing it myself. Where is your sister, the landlord asks. He is always at home. He is at home a lot. On his phone. If he is not at home he is on his boat. Where is your sister, the landlord asks. I don't know what materials my sister is using for the cistern. The maintenance man must have given her some. A piece of the loaf. I tell the landlord that my sister is sick.

Some tenants don't stay at Slater Mill. They feel sick, they say.
The riverview is not a good thing at Slater Mill. The river does
not move. It stains the rocks blue. Sick is sick. Sick is not well
and not dying. Sick is so clear. And also not. We don't know
what our own blood is doing when it is buried inside our bodies. The 1st baby, that was a shame. The poor parents, my sister
and I said. Burials are expensive and money is dear. And babies
are dear. The 2nd baby died and my sister got the idea about
the water. Seepage. Though the landlord said it was the air.
The baby was blue-faced. One said water, one said air. Now
the 3rd baby. I have given the orchard ground a lot of thought.
It will not work to break up the cement. The ground is unnatural underneath. Wet and bleeding. A sticky blue. What kind
of orchard would grow from that ground. It is a thing of night-
mares. My dream of the pear, of the pear and its blue flesh, is
a warning. It is also, to me, a yes. A yes to my plan. It will not
work to break up the cement. I need to make new dirt. I need
to make new dirt and I am making new dirt. I have given the
orchard ground a lot of thought. It is I who empty all the trash
bins into the dumpster. It is lucky that this is my job. I am in the
dumpster area all the time. All the time now, I am making dirt.
The orchard needs many feet of ground. It will all need to be
new dirt. Nothing under the cement is natural or good.

Sundays I am making an orchard. It is a good thing for me. It is a good day. Mondays we clean, and Tuesdays and Wednesdays. Thursday is linens. Fridays and Saturdays we clean. With rags and mopheads. We spray bottles of poison on the windows, on the banisters, on the floors. I spray bottles of poison into the bins after I empty them. Hold your breath, my sister says. This is poison, my sister says. She cares about seepage. She has asked the landlord for gloves. She says what we spray to clean is poison spray. She has asked the landlord for gloves and for face masks. She cares about seepage. My sister thinks living things want to live. She thinks about what is in the water, what is in the air. All I care about is what is in my ground. I am angry with my sister. With her plans for a cistern. With her asking the landlord for gloves and for face masks. I do not want the landlord to think about me and my sister. I do not want him to think about the noises on the roof. I do not want him to think about the noises in the dumpster area. There is an orchard there and the landlord must not see it. He will not see it unless he comes looking. The fence around the dumpster area is very high. The orchard is a good thing for me. There is seepage. The water is making the babies die. We are spraying the air with poison, my sister says. We are poisoning what we are trying to clean. It is funny. My sister has asked the landlord for gloves. If you ask the landlord for something you are asking for a piece of his loaf. My sister says the air is not his and the water is not his. Only the land, and there is no land. Only the mill, and the Now Leasing flag is up every day but Thursday. The orchard is such a good thing for me. To be making dirt. I do not want the landlord to think about my sister and me. No one but me should go into the dumpster area. No one should call the orchard Slater Orchard but me. The things I am making dirt from: the blue dictionary, fruit cores from the trash bins, the 3rd baby. Living things want to live and dead things want to live too.

Today is Sunday. Today is Sunday but I do not have anything
good. The landlord has asked my sister to go with him on a
tour of his property. He says it is time he tours his property.
To check on things, he says. He says tour and check on but he
means inspect. He means that he has thought about my sister
and me. His linens are clean and his bins are empty. But. He is
thinking about my sister and me and especially my sister. I am
not angry with her anymore. She thinks about seepage. A 4th
baby has died. My sister cares about what is in the water. I do
not. I do care about the ground. But I am trying to care less.
The landlord has made my sister take his arm. I watched them
go up the stairwell. She had to take his arm. At the middle of
the stairwell he stopped. We always clean the banisters. And
we mop the stairs. The corners get dirt stuck in them. We use
a knife to unbury the dirt from the stair corners. Then the wet
mophead drinks the dirt. And then we put the mophead back
in the bucket of water and the dirt seeps into the water. Then
I, and not my sister, who is not as strong as I, empty the mop
bucket into the big sink. And the water and its dirt go down
the drain. The drain does not smell good. The stairwells smell
good because we have sprayed the poison on them. The dirt
has been unburied and drunk up by the mophead and we have
sprayed the poison. And the smell of the poison will tell the
landlord that the stairwell is clean.

The landlord made my sister take his arm. He is inspecting his property. I do not want to think about his arms or about his eyes squinting at his property. My sister and I clean well. But we have our projects. My sister, I know, will protect her cistern. The landlord will not see it. My sister is the unafraid one. I should have told her about my project. Our projects are not unlike after all. My sister and I are both thinking forwardly. We are thinking forward. We have projects. And now the parents of the 4th baby are knocking on my apartment door. It is a strange Sunday. Tenants never knock on the door of the apartment my sister and I live in. Our names are not on it. If there is a spill or something to be cleaned the tenants will knock on the maintenance man's door. And then he will tell my sister and me and we will clean it up. Now is not a good time for tenants to be knocking on our door. The landlord is touring his property. He has made my sister take his arm. Already the landlord is thinking about me and my sister. These tenants knocking on the door are the parents of the 4th baby to die. The 4th baby died yesterday. It is easy to know now when a baby has died here. The wailing of the parents can be heard in the stairwells. Other tenants will start to stand in the hallway near the apartment of the dead baby. I knew the 4th baby had died yesterday but I did not know the parents would knock on my apartment door. Money is dear. Babies are dear too. But. The landlord asks for a lot of money to lease an apartment here. The parents of the 4th baby to die must have talked to the parents of the 3rd baby. And now they are knocking on my door.

The landlord has made my sister take his arm. I do not know which part of Slater Mill he is inspecting right now. The parents of the 4th baby want to come into my and my sister's apartment. They must have talked to the parents of the 3rd baby. The 3rd baby to die is part of the ground of my orchard. The ground of my orchard is made of only good things. The dictionary, the fruit, the 3rd baby. It is taking a long time to make enough good dirt. I need at least a few feet of ground above the cement. It will take a long time. If I think about the exact components of the new dirt I will get distracted. Overall it is good dirt made from good things. Words and fruit and baby. It will make ground that is alive and not dead. But the landlord seeing my ground would not be good. It would poison the ground. To me, the ground would be poisoned if the landlord's eyes looked at it. The parents of the 4th baby have talked with the parents of the 3rd baby. And now they are here. It is natural they would think to ask me. The dumpster area is my place. I am always emptying the bins. I run the incinerator and I drag the dumpsters out to the curb when the truck arrives. The truck comes to empty the dumpsters once a week. There should be a schedule but there is not. I am always listening for the truck. I am in the dumpster area a lot. It is natural for the parents to think of me. Burial here is not easy. Mills go on for miles. The river does not move. Anything dropped in the river would not wash away.

The parents of the 4th baby are inside my apartment. They are crying. I was right to let them inside. The landlord is inspecting his property. And a cry is a call. Rude not to listen. If someone is crying, that is a call. The parents of the 4th baby are here. The 4th baby is here too. It was a boy. I am not comfortable with boys. Even baby ones. This one is in a towel. Its face skin is blue. I will not forget to tell my sister. Maybe the landlord is right. It was the air. The parents of this 4th baby to die are troubling me. They want me to bury the baby. They want to come with me to the dumpster area. I can't allow that. They are crying and they are cursing the cement. The cement does make it all worse. It does go on for miles. But cement is different to me now. It is keeping what is unnatural underground. Though there is seepage. A 4th baby has died. It would be better to curse the cement for not going far enough. If the cement finally covered the river too. This is something I had not thought through before. I have always thought less cement would be good. Maybe more cement is what we need. Keep the dead ground buried. Keep the dead water buried. The parents want to come to the dumpster area with me. My sister has always been the unafraid one. The word orchard is in my mouth. I have never said the word orchard aloud. It is my one good thing. Not even my sister knows of my project. Cry is a call. It is rude not to listen and rude not to answer. I tell the parents of the 4th baby about Slater Orchard. I also tell them about my nightmare, and how the flesh of the pears was blue. It was a horror to me in my dream. When I tell the parents of the 4th baby about the blue flesh, I tell it as if it were a good dream. Maybe it was a good dream. After all. I talk about the blue flesh of the pears in Slater Orchard as if it were a good dream. When I was inside the dream, I felt horror. The pears looked natural, but they were not. The flesh was blue. Sick is sick. The poison had seeped into my new dirt. The 4th baby was a boy and it was blue-faced. Now the parents know about my orchard. They are letting me take the 4th baby to the dumpster area by myself. They are crying when they leave the apartment I share with my sister. They are crying as they leave their baby. I will leave a basket of pears from Slater Orchard by their apartment door. It may take a long time for me to do this. Maybe years. The Now Leasing flag at Slater Mill is always flying because people are always leaving. Pears and years are in my mouth as the parents are leaving. Also leaving and leasing. My ground will be good. Leaving and leasing. And pears and years. If you hear crying, it is a call. Lease comes from leave, and it leads to leaving. But leave comes from staying. I do not know whether the parents of the 4th baby will stay. As they are leaving they say they will stay until Slater Orchard is real. But it is already real, so they may leave at any time.

If a river of cement could cover the air too. If everything could be cement except Slater Mill itself. The baby's face skin is blue. Maybe the landlord is right. It was the air. Poison is a drink. We are drinking it through the windows. Through the cracks in the walls. The ground of my orchard is made of only good things. Ash from the pages of the blue dictionary. Dirt I am growing from the fruit cores and fruit peels in the landlord's bins. It is taking a long time to make enough good dirt. The 3rd and 4th babies are part of the dirt. All the parts fit together well. And good is what fits. The parents of the 4th baby have left me a gift. They have left the gift outside the door of the apartment I share with my sister. Who knows nothing of my project. The gift is a paper torn from a dictionary. I burnt my blue dictionary. I wanted my orchard to have good ground. The parents of the 4th baby must have a dictionary too, only it is without this particular entry now. My sister is on a tour of the landlord's property again. She has taken his arm. This is the 3rd Sunday they have toured the property. I do not think I can tell my sister about my project now. It may be that she is taking the landlord's arm to show him how she and he fit together. She may be showing the landlord how she and he fit together so that she does not need to show him her cistern on the roof. But when I ask my sister how the landlord is, she smiles. She is still young enough to have babies. And a smile is below a laugh. It is hard to know whether I can tell my sister things now. I am not comfortable with boys and my sister knows that. The 4th baby to die was a boy. Now it is ground. I am supposed to give the parents a basket of pears with blue flesh. They will eat the blue flesh of the pears and their baby will be with them again. Or maybe not. It will take years. To thank me they have left me a page from their dictionary. But they have made a mistake. It is the way people say orchard in this area. It sounds like chid. Like someone has just been scolded. It sounds like it is spelled or-chid. That's the way people in this area say it. The parents of the 4th baby have given me the orchid entry from their dictionary. They mean it as a gift. Burials here are so difficult and money is dear. They must have been pleased to read the entry. It is about the orchid flower. Flowers must have seemed fitting to them. But it is not about an orchard. The baby was a boy and orchid is a testicle. They must have been pleased to read the entry. It must have seemed fitting. I do not have anything but the word orchard in my mouth, and it is in my mouth in a rich and round way.

Now a strange cry is coming from my orchard ground. I have
been so dumb. I have been so dumb. A cry is a call. You must
listen. But babies cry often. Babies are known for their cry. A
cry is a call and you must answer. But babies are babble. Foreign or strange. I cannot hear within the crying the meaning
of the cry. We do not know, my sister said, weeks ago now, we
do not know what the blood is doing when it is buried in our
own bodies. A strange cry is coming from my orchard ground.
We do not know what buried blood is doing. I have been so
dumb. These weeks have been weeks of crying. The parents of
the 5th, 6th, and 7th babies. Yes. Also, my sister. Crying, yes. I
have heard my sister crying in the laundry room. And I have
been dumb. The cries of the dumpster truck brakes. There
should be a schedule for when the dumpster truck comes.
There should be a schedule but there is not. I have to listen out
for the truck's brakes. At all times I must listen out. It is a cry
that they have. The brakes call me and I run to the dumpster
area. I run and unlatch the gate and roll the 3 dumpsters to the
courtyard to be emptied. There are 4 dumpsters in the area.
I roll only 3 every time. Inside the 4th is where I am making
new dirt. I am making new dirt and I am nearly done. The 4th
dumpster has dirt up to its lid. It is hiding dirt inside itself. Its
pile of dirt is waist-high and wider than my body is long. I have
made new ground and no one must know. The parents of the
4th, 5th, 6th, and 7th babies know. But they are no one. They
have babies in the ground. The parents of the 4th, 5th, 6th,
and 7th babies know but they are no one now. They are here

but not here. No one must know and they are no one now. The 3rd baby is also part of my dirt but its parents don't know that it is. I did not tell them how I would bury that baby. All the parents are dumb. It's the dumpster truck driver who is supposed to unlatch the gate. He is supposed to drive his truck right up to the dumpster area. That is what the landlord supposes he does. That is what the landlord pays him a piece of the loaf to do. I have never said anything to the dumpster truck driver. He and I have never spoken. We never speak.

The cistern is finished. Now on the roof of Slater Mill is a cistern. Its water comes from the sky. It is on a raised platform. A raised platform on a high roof. There can be no seepage. I am happy for my sister and her cistern. The maintenance man helped her. Seven babies have died. Now there is a cistern on the roof. If more babies are born, they will not die. I have to listen out for the dumpster truck's brakes. It is a cry they have. It is hard to listen out in the laundry room. And hard to listen out when vacuuming. Mondays, Tuesdays, Wednesdays, Fridays are vacuuming days. It is hard to listen out then. It is also easy to mistake one cry for another then. Thursdays is linens and it is hard to listen out then too. I cannot relax in the laundry room. It is so hard to listen out in that room. And now the laundry room is where my sister cries. Thursday is linens and my sister does not cry then. But I have heard my sister crying in the laundry room. On other days. Sundays. And I have been dumb. Her cry sticks to the walls of the laundry room. I hear it on Thursdays. On Thursdays, it is funny. There is my sister in the laundry room with me and she is talking to me and laughing at me and at the same time I can hear her cry. Her cry is stuck to the walls. I have to listen out all the time for the truck's brakes. The dumpster truck driver and I have never spoken. It is hard to listen out all the time. There should be a schedule. But there is not. The landlord makes my sister take his arm on Saturdays too now. The cistern is finished. My sister has her cistern and still on Saturdays and Sundays she is taking the landlord's arm. The kinds of cries at Slater Mill are the dumpster truck's brakes, my sister's laundry-room cry, the wailing of the parents of babies who have died, which can be heard in the stairwells, and a cry that is foreign or strange coming from my orchard ground.

AND NOW THE RIVER HAS STARTED MOVING AGAIN. The river is poison. The mills killed it and its bend. The parents of the babies who have died did not use the river for burials because the river did not move. Its water stains the rocks blue. The ground beneath the cement is bleeding and the blood is blue. Seepage, my sister says. Though she also says we don't know what the blood is doing in our own bodies. Now the river is moving. I have always wanted the river to move. It is natural that it should move. But the river moving is not good. It is not good. Now there is a new seepage. The air is definitely poison now. The river moves and the poison flies into the air. And now there is noise. The river makes a noise as it moves. It is hard for me to listen out for the cries. The river is moving and it is not good. And now I have had a 2nd dream. I dreamt of blood, blood in a very neat channel. The blood did not spill out of its very neat channel. In the dream I was watching the blood move in its channel. Then I took a step back and saw that there were more channels. There were seven channels and the blood was moving in them. I took a second step back and saw that the channels were buried in my orchard ground. Not in the dead ground. Not in the dead ground underneath the cement but in the new dirt that I had made from true things. I would have liked to have had this dream afterward, after the river started moving again. If I had had the dream afterward, it would have felt more natural. It is natural to see a river move and then to dream of blood moving in a channel. What you dream being born from what you see. It is so natural for the mind to re-mind itself. Of how blood is like water. How the word blood was born from water. That which bursts. Only, the river did not move in the days before my dream. It is so natural to see a river move and then to dream of blood moving. What you dream being born from what you see. Or what you fear being born from where you hurt. But it is not like that here.

In the dream I watched the blood move in its channel. Which is a bed. A channel is a bed. For what is at rest, for what does not move. What is dead. There were seven channels in my dream and seven babies have died so far. But only five were buried in my orchard ground. What is dead is asleep. A channel is a bed. My thinking isn't bringing me anyplace. Cries, strange and foreign, are coming from the orchard ground. I can't think my way to what is true. The day after the 2nd dream, the river began moving again. Which was not natural. When I awoke, I had fear. I had fear though I had not yet been hurt. And my sister was not in her bed.

It is not my sister's fault that the 8th baby has died. She built a cistern on the roof. She thought the water was the problem. If the parents and the baby had only had clean water. My sister and I both thought the water was poison. The 8th baby was born with cysts. We heard the tenants talking softly outside the parents' door. Cysts. Cysts on the face. My sister and I both thought the well water was poison. And it was. When the parents popped the cysts, a blue pus flowed forth. We both thought the cistern water was clean. It was not. The river started moving again. Its poison seeped into the air. The rain fell right through the river's seepage. Though maybe the cistern water was cleaner than the well water. The 8th baby to die did not have blue skin on its face. It did not have blue skin but it did have cysts and from the cysts a blue pus flowed. So the cistern water was a little cleaner. But in the end it did not matter. And it is funny how the landlord was right. It was the air he said. He said this because the air is not his. He loves for my sister and me to spray poison into the air. The smell of poison means clean to him. He does not know that poison is a drink.

Saturdays is windows. So many things are grieving me that I find it difficult to move. The windows of Slater Mill flip open. We can wipe both sides of the glass from inside the mill. I am finding it difficult to move. The river is moving again. When my sister and I flip the windows the poison air comes in. So many things are grieving me. The windows of the 3rd floor stairwell look onto the dumpster area. Things are moving with my orchard. But the windows of the 3rd floor stairwell are a problem. I would like them to stay clouded over. My sister and I split the job of windows. The back stairwell is mine. It's mine and I can keep one window clouded over. Which is a relief. It is a relief but I do not feel relieved. I have not been relieved of my sister's crying. Nor of the cries, strange and foreign, coming from my orchard ground. And I need to listen all the time for the brakes of the dumpster truck. If the truck were to come and I did not hear it . . . Many things are grieving me. And now my sister is asking if I'm going to bury the 8th baby in my garden. She is calling my orchard a garden. I did not tell my sister about my project but she knows. And I thought that my ground would be good. I thought that I could protect the dirt from the air. The dirt is in the 3rd and 4th dumpsters right now. It is protected from the air right now. But when I spill it onto the ground to make my orchard, the air will touch it. I am not sure the air will not poison it. I have so much dirt that the 3rd dumpster is nearly full too. I have to listen all the time for the truck's brakes. And now my sister is asking me about the 8th baby. And now she is going off to take the landlord's arm. And the river is moving again and its poison hangs in the air. And where are the face masks and gloves that my sister, the unafraid one, has asked for.

The 3rd and 4th dumpsters are both nearly full of new dirt. Many things are grieving me and yet my orchard is not heavy to me. The dumpster truck driver arrives. I hear the cry of his brakes. It is a call. I run to unlatch the dumpster area gate. I pull the 1st and 2nd dumpsters down to the curb. I get into the cab of the truck. The dumpster truck driver is old so he does not mind as much that I am old too. He does not seem to mind that my skin smells like the poison that my sister and I spray as we clean. There ought to be a schedule. If there were I might try to be cleaner. But there is not a schedule and the dumpster truck driver does not seem to mind the smell of poison on me. And I do not mind lying down in the cab of his truck. I do not like his hair or his testicles, but I do not mind lying down in his truck. Testicles are ugly and I do not like boys. My sister would laugh if she saw me in the cab of the truck. My sister and I have both always said that testicles make the whole thing look messy. We would remove the testicles if it were up to us, my sister and I used to say. Just lop them off and the whole thing would look cleaner. I am not comfortable with boys, and testicles make the whole thing messy. Lop them off and the whole thing would be cleaner. But now that I have seen the testicles of the dumpster truck driver I have a different opinion. I have a different opinion but it is still not a good opinion. Testicles are the witnesses. They are true to their name. Testicles are the witnesses, and my opinion is not a good one. I do not mind lying down in the cab of his truck. Actually it is a pleasure to lie down in the middle of a work day. It is a pleasure to lie down.

It is also a pleasure to laugh at the testicles bearing witness. I do not like boys and do not know many. Only the landlord, the maintenance man, and the dumpster truck driver. But it feels true to say that boys need a witness. Two witnesses. My opinion of testicles is not good. And then after the 8th baby died I also thought cysts. Two cysts. Twins. I also thought of popping the testicles. They looked like cysts. I thought of popping them to see if blue pus would flow forth. But I did not pop them. The dumpster truck driver has his witnesses.

It is time to start the seedlings. My orchard will need to be babied. I will not throw the seeds onto the ground. Even if that is the natural way. It might be natural for an orchard to be born by seeds thrown onto the ground, but that is not the way I am making my orchard. I am making my orchard in a way that is natural to me. It is natural for me to make an orchard this way. To grow clean dirt, and to hide the clean dirt in the dumpsters. To grow clean dirt out of fruit cores and pages of the blue dictionary and organic material from the babies who have died. My dirt will be true. Deht is how we say it. Deht. No r. The r would make the word shallow. The word would not go as deep into our mouths if we said the r. Dirt. I know how it is spelled and I know how it is said. Deht I say. I say it that way even in my head. My deht will be true. And pear trees are true to the feelings of this place. Which is autumnal. And it is right to baby the orchard. To start the seedlings inside. This is the only way to make an orchard at Slater Mill.

Making an orchard is really a natural thing for me to do. As natural as breathing or drinking. Which is funny. The air and water are poison. So breathing and drinking are not natural anymore. Or they are natural, but they are poison. And natural is born to it. And so we are born to poison. Though the tenants do drink tea. All the tenants are tea drinkers. Nearly every bin has tea bags and nearly every bin on one day each month has an empty tea box. The Now Leasing flag is always flying. Some tenants do not stay long. The air is not good. And the water is not good. The tenants drink tea instead. They think boiling the water will kill the poison. But maybe the poison is natural. We were born to it. The tenants drink their tea. Tea is leaves stripped from trees. And autumn is a stripped-down thought. So it is natural and good to start my orchard in tea boxes. It is natural to start and end a tree in a box. The box is born to it.

The dumpster truck driver and I never speak. We never speak. The 3rd and 4th dumpsters are nearly full of new dirt. They cannot be emptied. I moved my hands. I was on the curb and the dumpster truck driver was in the cab of the truck. The motor was running. I could not speak because the motor was running. It is very loud. I moved my hands. I made my hands say that the 3rd and 4th dumpsters were empty. Empty, my hands said. The driver moved his hands. The way he moved his hands fit the way I moved my hands. It was not the same way. But his way fit my way. What is good is what fits. That is all that good is. My hands moved across my body. They moved to say that the two dumpsters were empty. It is funny how that can mean something else. Funny and fitting. Good. Good. I am making an orchard. The river is poison. The cement goes on for miles. And I am making an orchard and that is so good. What happens to me and around me as I make the orchard is also good. It will fit. I am making new dirt. Now that the river is moving again the air is definitely poison. And the water is poison. I will need to cover my new dirt for as long as possible to keep it clean. A face mask for the dirt. Though I no longer wish for a face mask for myself. It was my sister's wish. She is unafraid, except for the poison. I am also becoming unafraid. I am making new dirt and I want it to be good. I no longer wish for a face mask. A mask is a mockery. The poison is everywhere. When I lie down in the cab of the dumpster truck the engine is running. The fumes fill the cab. I open my mouth. Poison is a drink. I open my mouth and poison runs down my throat.

Sometimes there is blood. I am old and so it is old blood. It
makes a small mess on the seat of the cab. It is old brown blood.
I don't know how long it has been in me. I don't know if it was
ever blue inside me. We don't know what our own blood is. It is
buried in our skin. When the dumpster truck man is buried in
my skin I am glad. I am glad that some of my blood is getting
out. I am glad I get to see the blood. Even if it is old. I am glad
to lie down in the middle of the day. I am glad to be touched.
Though I do not like boys. I do not like boys but I am glad to
be touched. I also like to laugh. The testicles are funny. They
are bearing witness and boys need witnesses. But it is also true
that I am glad my own body has a witness. It is good. Which
just means that it is fitting. One thing goes with the other. How
a word is a twin to the thing it means. Not the same, but fitting.
I open my mouth. Poison is a drink. But the word orchard is
always also in my mouth. The poison runs down my throat.
Orchard stays in my mouth.

I have been so dumb. I know dumb is from dust. But I do not know if dumb is dust in the eyes or dust in the mouth. Where did the dust go first, eyes or mouth. Dumb ends in the mind but where did it start. Dust in the eyes or dust in the mouth. It is not all one to me. When you have been so dumb you need to know where the dust got started. The landlord has ordered the incinerator to be turned off. Permanently, he says. Tenants are gathering outside an apartment on the 2nd floor. Another baby has died. I think it is the 9th baby. Slater Mill is crowded but usually quiet. It is easy to hear when the parents of a baby who has died are wailing. I can hear it in the stairwells. Another baby, the 9th, has died. But things will not proceed in the way that has become natural here. The 9th baby will not be part of my dirt. The landlord has ordered the incinerator off.

Oh why don't you grow lavender in your garden. This is what my sister has just said to me. The way we say lavender around here is laven-dear. I smile at my sister. Laven-dear is what I say back to her. There are many things I want to say to my sister and many things I do not want to say to her. There is a lot that is buried between my sister and me now. There are many things I do not want to say. Laven-dear is what I say to my sister. Her torso is long and fluid. A riverbend. Riverbend is a lonely word. It is not a word I say to my sister. My sister's cries are a call. They are a call that I do not answer. Her cries are stuck to the walls of the laundry room. Laven-dear is the smell of the detergent. Thursday is linens. I do not say to my sister that I am not surprised. Lonely is all one. *Oh, that's all one* is what people say when it does not matter. I do not say to my sister that it does not matter. I do not say that I am not surprised. I burnt every page from the blue dictionary. Now I can no longer look up lonely and that's all one and riverbend. A torso long and fluid like my sister's can be lonely. She is going to have a baby and I am not surprised. That's all one. All's one. I can no longer look up lonely. Or look down at my sister's torso and think lonely. That's all one. And all's one. There is something buried between all those words. Or I would not be surprised if something were buried between all those words. My sister is going to have a baby. I have been so dumb. Laven-dear is all I have said. Laven-dear is all I have said to my sister. I have said it as tenderly as I could. When I said laven-dear it was like I was giving a gentle chide. Wash, dear. Which is a funny thing to say to my sister, who cleans all day. And the 3rd and last dream I had at Slater Mill was also funny. It was funny in its way. In the 3rd and last dream I had at Slater Mill, my sister looked just like me. My sister was older. My sister was older and seemed more like cement. She was in the laundry room of Slater Mill and she was making a garden. I knew in the dream that she was making a garden, though there was no dirt. My sister is going to have a baby. On Sunday I was in the dumpster area. I looked up and saw a face in the 3rd floor stairwell window. It was looking down at me. When I told my sister about my 3rd and last dream at Slater Mill, she told me of her dream. Her dream was of fire, and of dust.

In my last dream, my sister was growing a garden of lavender.
I found her in the laundry room with cups of detergent. Lavender is the smell of the detergent we use on Thursdays. There
was a lot that was funny about the dream. In the dream I asked
my sister, who looked so much like me, What are you doing
with the detergent. And she said, Lye. I kept saying detergent
and she kept saying lye. We have never called detergent lye. It
is not a word we use. In the dream I tried so hard to figure out
what my sister was saying. I heard lie, and I thought that my
sister was telling me that my orchard ground was not good and
true. Then I remembered, in the dream, how my sister had
laughed at me when I mixed dye and die, and I knew that she
had said lye. Which is water. Water impregnated with ash. I
did not know then, in the dream, whether impregnated or ash
was the important part. I also still heard lie. The lights were
very bright in the laundry room and my sister looked as old
as I, which is too old to have babies. I was sorry my sister had
grown so old so quickly. She cleans all day. And what are you
doing, I asked her. And she said she was collecting lavender
from the lye. To plant in your garden, she said. She looked up
at me, in the dream, as she said this. The skin on her face was
blue. The dictionary I burnt at the start of my orchard was
blue. I wanted my orchard to be true so I burnt the dictionary.
Its ash was the start of my dirt. Now I know that was a mistake.
It was a big thing to do. I was showing off. I was showing off to
myself. But it was a mistake because I cannot know what is true
now. Is lavender a washing or is lavender a bluing. And what

are you doing, I asked my sister in the dream, with the lye. And my sister said, I am collecting its lavender. I saw a face looking down at me from the dumpster area. We say look up when we search for the truth of a word in the dictionary. In the dream when my sister looked up at me, her face was blue, and I knew then that my orchard was poison.

The landlord has ordered the incinerator off. My sister has had a dream of fire and dust. A lot is buried between us. The maintenance man has always been devoted to my sister. He helped her build the cistern. But it is the landlord's arm my sister takes on Saturdays and Sundays. So I do not know the circumstances of her baby. And I do not know if she has told the landlord of her fire dream. When the landlord ordered the incinerator off, I worried. That is all I need now, I worried. But now I think, Fine, it's all one to me. The incinerator is off. Things seem to be going fast. I had always wanted the river to start moving again, and it is. It is, but the moving is not a good thing. It turns out that the river moving is not good. It turns out that my orchard is poison. I do not know if my plans for the orchard will continue. When I lie down with the dumpster truck driver, I do not like the hair on his body. Afterward, I pick off the hairs from his body that have fallen onto mine. I always pick off each of his hairs. I keep them for the incinerator. I like to be clean. Now the incinerator is off. I would like to stop everything. To stop is to plug up. As if all of Slater Mill, all of the lord's loaf—the dumpster area, the riverbend, the laundry room, the Now Leasing flag—were in a big basin. To stop is to plug up with hemp. We don't have any hemp here. But we do have denim. My sister and I have seen piles of denim in odd places. We think Slater made denim here. I would like to stop everything. As if all of Slater Mill were in a big basin, and I was plugging up the drain of the basin with a piece of denim. I am wishing to flood everything. I am wishing for everything to end in water. But my sister had a dream of fire, and of dust. That is the difference between us.

It is Sunday now. I do not want to make an orchard anymore. My seedlings grow. My seedlings are growing though I do not water them. Living things want to live, my sister says. I do not water the seedlings because I am dumb. I have been so dumb. The water here is poison. The rainwater the riverwater the wellwater. There is nothing my orchard can be but poison. The maintenance man helped my sister build a cistern on the roof. The tenants could drink the cistern water and the babies would not die. Then the river started moving again and its poison seeped into the air. Then the rain was poison. Then the birds on the roof who had watched my sister build the cistern all died. It may have been the air. But they died in the cistern itself, so it may have been the water. Now there is also a mucus. In addition to cysts from which a blue pus flows forth, there is also a mucus. The tenants are getting a mucus in the throat that will not move. It is thick. All the tenants have a rasp because of the mucus. The maintenance man says it might be a bird disease, from the dead birds in the cistern. My sister doesn't say anything. She is discouraged. And she is going to have a baby. I would like to stop up everything until it is flooded. My sister said she dreamed of fire and dust but she will not say more.

It is funny how poisoned my orchard ground is. I had thought, My dirt is so good and true. It is so good. Which is funny now because I see the poison everywhere. The 3rd and 4th dumpsters really are full of dirt now. I have grown this dirt from trash and ash and fruit cores in the bins and from the organic material of the babies who have died. Funny is just befooled. It is so funny that I burnt the pages of my blue dictionary to make good dirt. Good and true and clean dirt. Funny is befooled. The pages of the dictionary were poison. They were not pure wood pulp. The pages were made into pages by poison. And the fruit that the landlord eats and throws into the bin is poison. It grew in poison ground and was sprayed with poison spray. The landlord asks my sister and me to spray the air with poison. He calls that cleaning. The fruit he eats is poison to the core. I grew my dirt from the poison cores. And the babies buried in my orchard ground are poison. They are pure poison. Which is a funny thing to say. Pure is the opposite of poison. But funny is just befooled. I looked up and saw a face in the 3rd floor stairwell window. A face was looking down on my orchard. And so my orchard is poisoned that way too. Things seem to be going fast. But nothing has happened. I can see that. Slater built this mill at the riverbend. After that, nothing happened. Nothing has happened. I said to my sister, Nothing has happened. Slater picked the nicest spot on the river. Its bend. After that nothing happened. The parents of the 9th baby to die have knocked on the door of the apartment I share with my sister. It is still Sunday. My sister is sitting. The seedlings are growing. The parents are knocking. My sister is sitting. The parents have brought their baby who has died. Free funerals are not a new idea. It's true that the landlord has ordered the incinerator off. But, nothing has happened. Slater built his mill and after that nothing happened. To let the parents inside is natural. To take the baby from them is natural. This baby is not a boy. This baby has the cysts filled with blue pus. Also it has the new problem. It has the mucus. Mucus is gluing its eyes shut. The parents say that it has mucus in its throat too. All the tenants are getting the mucus. The parents of this 9th baby want it buried with a small piece of paper. The paper, they say, is important. They say it has the baby's last words. The baby was born alive and rasped before it died. The baby was born alive and rasped before it died but I do not see that anything has happened. The dust must have started in my eyes. I no longer see that things have happened. To take the baby from the parents is natural. The small piece of paper is buried in its fist. Slater picked the nicest spot on the river. Its bend. After that nothing happened.

It is lucky the river has started moving again. It is actually very good that it has started moving. It is spraying its poison into the air but poison is not a new thing here. There is always room for more poison. It is very good that the river is moving. It is likely that the babies would die anyway. And likely that the birds would die too. The water in the cistern would have been poison anyway. The wood that the maintenance man gave to my sister was not just wood. It was not purely wood. Like how a word is not purely its meaning. Poison the pages to make the dictionary. Poison the wood to make it a page. Poison the wood to make it wood. The wood must have looked like a tree. At some point it looked like a tree. Then poison stripped its bark. Wood is an autumn thought. You must strip it from the tree. The wood is not the tree. It is the tree plus poison. Poison the wood to make it wood. Paint another poison over the wood. To drown it. The wood could not breathe. First its bark was stripped and then it could not breathe. Then, it looked like wood. The poison killed it and the poison made it. And then my sister and the maintenance man made a cistern with the poison wood. And the water sat in the bowl of poison wood all day. And we were to drink it. Seepage, my sister says. It is best not to think of it though. Or do think of it. Think of seepage and poison and water in a bowl of wood. Think and drink from the cistern, the well, the river. Nothing can happen. Nothing has happened. The water is fine to drink. It is as good as any water. It is as clean as anything. I open my mouth and drink it down. Nothing has happened. Except for the luck of the river, which has started moving again. It is lucky. I can put the 9th baby into the river and it will wash away. The landlord has ordered the incinerator off. The parents of the 9th baby put it into my hands. And I can put the baby into the river and it will move away. A water burial is as good as a ground burial.

A small piece of paper is buried in the fist of the 9th baby. Which was born alive. It was born alive and rasped before it died. I am feeling glad for this 9th baby. It was born alive and it rasped. A death rasp, but a rasp. It is all one. The parents wrote down the baby's words. They are not real words. I have dug into the fist of the 9th baby and read its words on the paper. They are not real words. But it's possible they are true. It's possible they are truer than real words. Nothing is buried beneath the 9th baby's words. I am glad for this 9th baby. It died. But it was born alive. And now the river will take it. I have put it in the river, and the river will move it. Maybe to the sea. It is dark out and I cannot see the 9th baby anymore but maybe its body will get to a sea. Nightmare. I do not mind being demoness of corpses. I am glad the 9th baby may get to the sea. I am glad that mare can be a sea. The mills go on for miles but mare can be a sea. I am very glad. I dug into the fist of the 9th baby and I read its vocables.

I am not sure if my sister and I were born alive. It is rare. It is maybe a rare thing. Slater built his mill and after that, nothing happened. I dug into the fist of the 9th baby for a piece of paper. I read its vocables. They were not real words. But they were true. I will put the paper with the 9th baby's vocables in my orchard. Yes I am still making an orchard. Yes there is always room for more poison. And what would an orchard of pure poison be. Would it be an orchard that grows poison. Or one that eats it. Or an orchard that is truly poison—a naked orchard that does not hide its poison. An orchard with cries coming from its ground.

It is lucky the river has started moving again. Saturdays is windows. It is a job my sister and I split. My sister sprays the poison. Then she steps back. She steps back quickly and does not
breathe. I step forward quickly and use one rag to wash the
window and one rag to dry it. The washing rag gets dirty fast.
It comes away from the window with a grime. Its smell is faint
but foul. And the grime is blue. My sister does not breathe.
It is funny. We are trying to protect her baby but it is funny.
Where is there not poison. Even my orchard. Even my orchard
will be pure poison. My sister and I like the moment when the
washing rag is plunged into clean water. The clean water eats
the grime. We like to watch that. But now there is so much blue
grime. The water is full. It is time for a new rag. It is time for
a new bucket of water. It is funny to even think that. A new
bucket of water. It is just the bleach that makes the new water
look clean. When I look into the bucket, the new water looks
so clean. I could drink it. But it is just the bleach. Don't look
into things. Look up words or look down. Someone has been
looking down on me and my orchard from the 3rd floor stairwell. Now it is Saturday and I am looking down at the river
from the 3rd floor hallway. The river water looks clean now
that it has started moving again. The landlord's boat moves in
the current. And it is funny that I had not thought of it before.
The landlord's boat. And the sea. Now I have a plan for my
sister and her baby. The river has started moving again. There
is a boat. The mills go on for miles. But there is a sea. There
might be a sea. A bucket of clean water eating the blue grime.

But my sister does not want to go. She does not want to look for a sea. She wants to stay here and not breathe. And also not drink. My sister is afraid now. We did not switch. I am not the unafraid one now. Now my sister is afraid and so am I. We do not think her body can eat all the poison. Already it is probably in the baby. How big of a bucket is my sister's body.

My sister and I do not speak anymore. It is the mucus. It is
stuck in all the tenants' throats. It will not move. It could be
from the dead birds in the cistern. But the landlord says it is
the air. He has ordered the incinerator off. What does that
mean. The landlord has ordered the incinerator off. I think
that means that the baby is his. Another piece of the loaf. It
is inside my sister but it is his. And he might want to take the
thing that is his inside my sister. On his boat. To the sea. The
landlord is always on the phone. He is always sitting and smoking and on the phone. He must know what is at the end of this
river. Maybe he is already making calls. Maybe the weather
keeps all the poisons only in this area. Maybe the weather and
the cement keep the poison locked here. It is true that there is
hardly ever any wind. I do not want my sister to leave. There
is a lot buried between us. But I will be glad if she leaves. I
want her to leave soon. By boat. Before there is too much poison in her body. And there is also the dumpster truck driver.
How a truck would get my sister to the sea is something I don't
know. But a truck could also help her leave. I don't know if it
would be better to have my sister on the boat with the river
poison everywhere or to have my sister in the cab of the truck
with its fumes. When we spray the windows, my sister does not
breathe. She could leave on a boat or a truck. And not breathe
for miles. When the dumpster truck driver looked at the 3rd
and 4th dumpsters, I tried to make the sign for empty with
my hands. Which was also the sign for full. I could make the
sign again. When the dumpster truck driver returns I could

make the sign again. Next to my sister's torso. The dumpster truck driver understands empty and full. To lie down or not. To breathe or not breathe. He understands each sign. Though each sign means something different to him.

Whatever happens to me when I am making my orchard is good. The incinerator is off, and I cannot burn the hairs that fall from the body of the dumpster truck driver onto my body. He leaves his hairs on my body. Now I have to pick each hair off and add it to the dirt. I like to be clean. That is a funny thing to say and a dumb thing to say. Actually I feel ashamed that I said that. I like to be clean. It is funny because I'm not sure what clean means. I want it to mean everything. I don't know what the word is that means everything and asks for everything and makes something happen. I should shut my mouth. My sister will not leave. Living things want to live is something my sister used to say. Living things want to live I remind her. I write it on a piece of paper and put it in her apron pocket. I know she has read it because the next day the paper is no longer in her pocket. My sister and I do not speak and also I do not see her. I really do not see her. Now that the incinerator is off there is the problem of the trash. Slater Mill has four dumpsters. But the 3rd and 4th dumpsters are filled with dirt. If there is more trash than the 1st and 2nd dumpsters can fit, I cannot burn it. All of the things that used to be alive, I put into my dirt. Even the paper, because it was a tree that was stripped. I especially like putting paper into my dirt. It is right that my orchard, which will be a bare, stripped orchard, should grow in dirt made of stripped trees. I am not looking into the poison that stripped the wood and bleached the pulp. The dirt can eat those. My dirt is true and good. The dirt will eat the poison. Dirt is another word whose meaning I do not know. I burned

the dictionary. It is funny that the important words like orchard
and dirt are the ones whose meanings I do not know. But funny
is befooled. And I am a fool. I have put everything into words
whose meanings I do not know. Or-charred. Deht. Now they
must mean everything I need them to mean. I am happy not to
have a dictionary. I am happy I cannot check. I would rather
be befooled. Right now orchard and dirt are good words. Good
and true. And I have plans for my sister to leave. I really do not
see her. Now that the incinerator is off there is the problem of
the trash. The 3rd and 4th dumpsters are filled with dirt. I am
sorting trash all the time now. I have not seen my sister. It is as
if she has already left. If my sister could leave, that would be
something that has happened. If her baby could not die. If
the baby could be born alive and speak. A baby is a babble. I
have put the paper with the 9th baby's vocables in my orchard
ground. The body of the 9th baby is in the river. I put the
baby in the river and its vocables in my orchard. The orchard
ground has cries coming from it. I listen out for the cries but I
do not know their meaning. The cries are strange and foreign
and a little bit grinding. I do not know their meaning. I am
hopeful. Right now I think the cries are a noise the dirt is
making as it grinds the poisons. The dirt is grinding up the
poisons inside itself. The poisons are being released from the
dirt as cries. Deht is how we say dirt. Like debt. What is owed
is not paid. The dirt is grinding up the poison inside itself.
What is owed is not paid. There is no poison in my orchard.
Right now that is what I think.

I am hopeful. When I am hopeful I am glad to clean. I am cleaning Slater Mill faster than ever. I do some of my sister's cleaning too. On Fridays I do all the stairwells. On Saturdays, all the windows. If my sister can leave, it will be good that she has not washed too many windows here. If my sister leaves, that would be something that has happened. The incinerator is turned off and the trash is a problem for me. There is trash that does not fit in the 1st and 2nd dumpsters. My job is to empty the bins. The 1st week the incinerator was off, I took any trash that used to be alive and put it in my orchard ground. I put the rest of it in the laundry room. I did not know if the dumpster truck driver would come before Thursday but he did. He did come and empty the 1st and 2nd dumpsters. I made the sign to him to wait. I did not know if he would see it as leave or as go. Even my hand out, my hand out saying stop could mean wait or it could mean you are done. You can go.

A 10th baby has died. We heard the wail of the parents. The landlord has stopped taking my sister's arm. He will not bring her on his boat. The 10th baby to die also had the cysts and the mucus, but it was not born alive. The mucus confuses me. My sister said it was from the dead birds in the cistern. The landlord said it was from the air. Mucus is seepage. Something seeping out of your body. Right now, there is mucus stuck in the tenants' throats. But I am hopeful. Mucus is seepage. Something is trying to seep out of the bodies of the tenants. Something is trying to leave. I think it is the poison that is trying to leave. I am hopeful. My sister will not leave with the landlord after all. But the river is moving. The 9th baby has moved down the river. And things are moving out of the tenants' bodies. I have asked the maintenance man to take my sister on the landlord's boat. Things are moving very fast. I am hopeful that something will happen. I have packed my sister's things. It will be hard to clean all of Slater Mill by myself. And to also make Slater Orchard. But if my sister could leave, something will have happened. The maintenance man is going to take my sister to the boat at night. It is best that way. At night the river has a blue tinge now. The poison is making it brighter and brighter. I am hopeful that they will take the boat all the way to the sea. It is possible that the poison is really just in this area. The mucus is a good thing. The mucus is a good thing. It is funny to say that. But it's possible that the mucus is poison trying to leave the body. It's possible that the cries coming from my orchard ground are the noise of the dirt as it grinds away the poison. But I have been so busy thinking about what is possible. So busy and so dumb. I have not looked into things. I have been afraid to really look into things. I have not looked into what leave means. Or change. They are not good words. Neither leave nor change is good, I don't think. They are not right and they are not everything. Orchard is right and everything but what else.

The 9th baby is still here.

The 9th baby is still here and now my sister will not leave.

At night the river is bright now. It is tinged blue. The poison is making it brighter. The poison is a light. It is funny to say that the poison is a light. It is funny to say that if I think about what light means. But I do not want to think. The 9th baby is still here. My sister will not leave. Nothing has happened. I had thought a water burial would be as good as a ground burial. The river is moving again. I had thought the 9th baby might get to the sea. Poison is a drink. It is also a light. The blue in the river is very bright at night. The maintenance man agreed to take my sister on the boat. The landlord no longer takes my sister's arm. But he might think that the baby she is going to have is his. He might think that what is inside of her is his. And the boat is his. Pieces of the loaf. I had packed my sister's things. I had asked the maintenance man to leave with her. I had thought they might get to a sea. The poison is not everywhere. Or yes, the poison is everywhere but there is a sea big enough to swallow it. Slater killed the river but it's possible there is a sea. I had thought. But the 9th baby. Nine sounds like none. Like neigh. The horse from the nightmare saying no. The 9th baby is a nightmare to me now. It is a nightmare to my sister too. And to the maintenance man. They were on the boat. They went so quietly. The river was moving. They were going to untie the ropes and float down the river. They did not know how to use the motor and they did not need it. The river is moving again. It is going somewhere. When I thought of the nightmare I had had, I thought, maybe mare is sea. They are taking a night boat to the sea. But the 9th baby was there. The 9th baby is still here. Nine is none, no, a neigh. Nightmare is horse. But also it is my fault. I buried the baby in the water. Demoness of corpses. The baby did not leave. Its body must have gotten stuck under the boat. The maintenance man and my sister stepped onto the boat. They were going to untie the ropes and leave. If there were not poison in the river they would not have seen what they saw. But that is silly to think. The poison is everywhere. You cannot think around it. The blue light of the river really is getting brighter at night. My sister and the maintenance man saw the 9th baby very clearly. Its body must have gotten stuck under the boat. The bodies of the maintenance man and my sister stepping onto the boat must have moved things. They saw the 9th baby very clearly in the water. It was bright blue. It was bright blue, my sister said. Really she rasped. The mucus is very thick. It was bright blue. She means the baby. But it was only the poison in the water lighting up the baby. It's funny to say that poison is a light. But nothing is happening and I think not even a joke can happen. Slater built his mill here. He killed the river. And after that, nothing happened. Poison is really the end of the story. You can't think around it. My sister has not left. She will not leave. The parents of the 10th baby are waiting outside my apartment door. The brakes of the dumpster truck are crying at the curb. Someone

has stolen the Now Leasing flag. The seedlings are big now and
ready to be planted.

STRANGE WEATHER. A wind filled with dust. A wind that has dried up the mucus in the tenants' throats. Now there is a cough. The mucus is dried up and now the tenants cough. But cough is what a cough sounds like. This new sickness sounds like a bark. It is a bark the wind has brought. The wind has dried up my sister's cries too. She no longer cries. She is unafraid again. She has been unafraid since the wind came. The 9th baby in the water was not a nightmare, she says. The 9th baby, she says, was a reminder. She does not say of what. I no longer know what is inside my sister's mind. I have not known. What I think is there is wrong. When I saw her drinking the detergent, I thought one thing, but I was wrong. My sister was in our apartment sitting. It was Thursday. Linens. I was doing the linens all alone. I delivered the landlord's clean linens to his apartment. Which is my sister's job. But the landlord did not ask me, Where is your sister. He was on the phone. He was on the phone and smoking. On the phone and touching the cigarette ash to the phone. He is on the phone a lot. I did all the linens alone. My sister was sitting. She has been sitting since the night of the 9th baby. Nothing has happened since that night. Nothing has happened since Slater built his mill. I did all the linens. Except the Now Leasing flag. It has been stolen. My sister and I used to think we knew all the secrets in Slater Mill. We clean all day. We clean all day and find the hidden things. And see and hear. But now we are dumb. Who stole the flag. Who is watching me in the dumpster area from the 3rd floor stairwell window. And what is in my sister's mind, I don't

know. I finished the linens and she was sitting and drinking a
blue drink. Poison. What is that, I asked. Detergent, she said.
It was Thursday. Thursday is linens. The detergent smells like
lavender and it is blue. She was drinking it. I thought she was
trying to clean the baby. She is drinking the detergent to clean
the baby. Thursday is linens. But she was trying to kill the baby.
To clean or to kill. She was killing. She is the unafraid one. Her
torso will be long and fluid again. But riverbend is lonely. To
me. My sister does not look down. She does not look up either.
She is finished with the roof and the cistern. Nothing can be
cleaned of the poison.

My sister's torso will be long and fluid again. But she is bleeding. The blood is blue. It could be the detergent washing out of
her. But it smells like blood and not like lavender. It is the baby
bleeding out of her. The blood is blue. I have sat with my sister
and looked at the blood. She is sitting a lot. Listen out for this
bleeding, she says. This is the sound of the baby being born,
she says. And she laughs. It is not a crazy laugh. She is right to
laugh. It is funny. We have been befooled. My sister sits while
blue blood seeps out of her. It is funny that we thought she
could have a baby. It is funny that we thought the baby might
be born alive. I don't think my sister and I were born alive. I
am not sure. The 9th baby was born alive and it rasped and its
parents wrote down its vocables. They buried the baby's vocables in its fist and then I unburied them and put them in my orchard. Because vocables are the truest words. Though they are
not really words, which is why they are true. Write down the
sounds of my baby being born, my sister says. And we laugh. It
is funny. I am dumb but good at listening out. I listen out and
the sound of the baby bleeding out of my sister sounds like a
drip. Not like a faucet drip. A thicker drip. Tlllg. If the tongue
made those sounds together. Tlllg. Put that in your garden, my
sister says, and she laughs, and I say, It is an orchard. That
might have been the last sentence I said to my sister. The wind
really was making it hard to talk. The wind had brought a bark.
Also I was busy with the trash. I couldn't burn it and didn't
know where to put it. The trash was taking all of my time. Also
I have been doing all of my sister's cleaning. Slater Mill is the

biggest of the mills. There is so much to clean. And now the wind makes everything worse. It is blowing the poison dust in through the cracks. The vacuum is always clogged now. The water bucket must be emptied all the time. It is hard to mop. The dust that the wind blows in does not have a smell when it is dry. But when it is wet there is a bad smell. I cannot breathe through my nose. Also I am afraid. Someone has been watching me from the 3rd floor stairwell window. I have not cleaned that window. I have left it cloudy on purpose. Still, someone can see. I am afraid it is the landlord. He no longer takes my sister's arm. Did he know about the baby. He ordered the incinerator off. Was that to stop the trash burning or to stop the burning of the body of the baby. The baby that was inside my sister that he might have thought his. And if it was his, that baby was only made because my sister wanted to show the landlord how she and he fit together. So that she would not have to show him the roof. Her cistern was going to be something that could happen. But then the river started moving again. My sister and the landlord were an exchange. Not the exchange the landlord thought. Or maybe. Maybe they were not the exchange my sister thought. I am afraid now. Strange weather and there is a fear in me. In me, in my blood. As if all the poison were getting ready for something. But nothing has happened. And now I am passing the maintenance man in the stairwell. Hold on, he says. To me, I think. The maintenance man does not say much, usually. Hold on is the most he has ever said to me. If he said it to me. It is hard to tell when he is talking who exactly he means to talk to. He looks down. And his voice is low. His voice is a lying down voice. His voice thinks that the ground is where it belongs. When he talks his eyes are on the ground and his voice is on the ground. Hold on, he said. But he kept walking. I don't know if he meant stop. He may have meant stop. Or he may have meant keep going. If he was talking to me. It is hard to tell. But hold on is just what I wanted someone to say to me. Which is funny. Because he may have meant stop. Or he may have meant keep going. Which is like saying nothing at all. What he said has cancelled itself. Stop or keep going. That is in my head all day. Should I stop or keep going. Nothing has happened. Since Slater built his mill nothing has happened. I am not really doing anything. Nothing can be done. I clean all day and I have buried tenants' babies but nothing has happened. I am making an orchard, yes, but that is nothing anymore either. The poison is everywhere. Still. Still. Hold on is what I wanted someone to say to me. It is just the thing I wanted someone to say. Hold on, the maintenance man said. Which was saying nothing. Which cancelled itself. It is really the perfect thing to say. And perfect is the end. Hold on is the thing to say at the end. Which is to stop or to keep going. If the maintenance man was talking to me. If he was talking to me I don't know what he meant but I know he meant my orchard.

Strange weather. The wind is a dry wind. It has brought a bark.
The tenants are barking all night. *Cough* is what a cough sounds
like. It is a bark this wind has brought. It is very hard to sleep. I
had always thought it would be nice to have a wind blowing. To
be in the mill and hear the wind blowing outside. But it is not
like that. The night is full of barks. And there is a fear in me.
All the poison in my blood is getting ready. Now there is a fear
that almost always runs through me. It is funny that the Now
Leasing flag has been stolen. It had always dripped off the rope.
Now there is wind. The flag would really have been flying. It
would have made a flapping noise all night. All night the landlord's boat slaps the water. If the Now Leasing flag had not
been stolen, it would flap in the wind all night. I had always
thought that would be nice. But now there is the barking. The
tenants barking all night. My sister and I too. In the stairwells
the barks are very loud. The barks sound like motors trying to
start. Motors trying to start and then dying. The 10th baby to
die is in the 4th dumpster. I had to bury its body whole. I could
not use fire or water. Its whole body is in the 4th dumpster. The
landlord is on the phone all the time now. He is never not on
the phone. And smoking. He stops talking when I am cleaning
his apartment. He moves into the hallway with his phone and
starts talking again. He has the bark too. The bark is living at
Slater Mill. The bark is in all the apartments. Even the landlord's. The air is very dry. It is adding a kk feeling to everything.
The landlord is on the phone all the time. What he has to say I
don't know. There is nothing to say. But he talks and barks.

This dry air adds a kk feeling to everything. When I am vacuuming I find my mouth making the kk. And everything in my head ends in a kk. The 9th baby born alive. Coo, I try to say but I say cock. The maintenance man saying, Hold on. Hold on. I try to say whoa. But I say work. Making an orchard out of new dirt. Out of what is true. But true goes to truck. The dry air adding a kk to everything. When I turn the vacuum off, I hear the cry of the truck's brakes. I cannot run to the curb. The landlord's apartment is not done being cleaned. My sister is sitting today. I am doing her cleaning too. My sister's job is dusting. It looks easy but it is not. With the wind, dusting is very difficult. The brakes are crying. When I finally can run to the curb, there is the dumpster truck driver. There is no truck. It is he who is crying. His crying sounds like his brakes. It sounds just like his brakes. Without a truck, I don't know how there can be a lying down. The driver has the bark too. It must be everywhere. There must be no place to get to that the poison does not reach. I had thought of the dumpster truck driver taking my sister and her baby in his truck. I had thought there would be a place he could take them in his truck. It was nice to think that there was another way for my sister to leave. If not by water, then by land. Though she did not leave. My sister is sitting and her baby is tlllg and it is funny I ever had that plan. And now the driver has no truck. I should not stand here with him if he has no truck. It is Monday, and Mondays are for cleaning the 3rd floor. The driver is crying and barking. He does not look good. I had thought that the dumpster truck driver would be a help. I had thought that when I was ready, he could help me tip over the dumpsters and spread the dirt. To

really start the orchard. I had thought he would be a way for
my sister to leave. But now he has no truck. He does not look
good. His look does not fit. Lying down is good. And good
means fitting. Making an orchard is good. It is only fitting to
make something at a mill. But the dumpster truck driver does
not look good. His face does not fit. Sick is sick. Sick is just a
way to live. But his look does not fit living. He does not look
good at all. The fear almost always runs through me now. I
have found bird feathers in the maintenance man's bin. All
night the tenants bark. In my 1st dream, there were 16 pear
trees in my orchard and I had thought, Oh, 16 babies will die.
It was easy to think the dream meant that. But 10 babies have
died. I cannot count my sister's because there was no body. I do
not think I can count my sister's baby, which was just blue dripping out of her. Now no babies are dying. None are being
born. Sick is sick. It is a way to live. The driver does not have a
good look. I can see why he is here. He and I have never spoken. I had thought that was a good thing. Such a good true
thing, I had thought. We made signs with our hands. And one
sign meant two things. And then we would lie down across the
two meanings. We would lie across them and connect them.
Which is funny. Which is funny now. I had buried the hairs
from his body. The hairs I had found on my skin afterward. His
hairs are part of my orchard ground. We have never spoken. I
have been dumb. Now he is sick and there is no truck. He
would speak if he could. But I can see why he is here. I am not
making a graveyard! I am making an orchard. Orchard and
graveyard cannot mean the same thing. Though they both
have ard. Is ard the idea of garden. Both have the idea of a

piece of land. Both words are funny then, because there is no land here. Or maybe the ard of orchard and graveyard is like the ard of hazard. Maybe they are both games. Like hazard is a game. It is a game with two dice. Or one. Die. Or maybe orchard and graveyard are both ard like bastard and coward. The blue dictionary was the first thing I burned. I have been dumb since then. The dumpster truck driver and I have never spoken. I will speak first. *Ard.* I think it is a question. Ard. Does he know what it means. He says back to me, *Hard.* It is a rasp. It is a rasp and also he has an accent. He is not from around here. He might not know the words we use around here. He said to me hard. And I can tell that he does not know what hard means. What hard means here. Which is strong. I spoke first. Ard, I said. I think it was a question. The dumpster truck driver said to me hard. I was very happy. Hard is strong. I had forgotten. I should not have been standing by the curb. Mondays are for cleaning the 3rd floor. But I was very happy. The dumpster truck driver could give me more words. He was not from around here. He must know new words. Hard, he said to me. Which is the last half of orchard. I am not making a graveyard! But the dry wind. The kk feeling. The kk sounds. The kk sound of the dumpster truck driver as he lit himself on fire. He said hard and then he lit himself on fire. The kk feeling and its sounds. He was very sick. Sick is sick. But sick can be too much. Around here sick is sick. You are not dead or dying. You are not alive much. Just sick. The dumpster truck driver said hard. He was not from here and he had new words. Or different meanings for the same words. I was very happy. I thought he would help me know what is true. And then he lit himself on fire. The kk feeling of the wind. The kk sound the fire made with his body. His body was very dry. It must have been very dry. He is all ash now. No bones. I found bird feathers in the maintenance man's bin. No bones there either. I think the dumpster truck driver wanted his ash to go in my orchard. Or to blow away in the wind. He lit himself on fire on the curb at my feet. I am not sure what I am meant to do. But I have his lighter. It fell at my feet. I have his lighter. A small incinerator. He gave me a small incinerator. I have an incinerator again. I see now. I also see sick. Sick is sick. But sick can be too much. It can be too much. The dumpster truck driver was crying and barking. I am not making a graveyard! There was no truck. I am not sure how to lie across what he may have meant. He is all ash now. Ash for the wind or for the orchard. And he is good and true. He said to me, Hard. Which is the last half of orchard. And he was not from here. Sick was not just sick. I took off a shoe and I put my foot inside his ash.

My sister is standing. All the blue has bled out of her. When I saw her drinking the detergent I thought of her baby. To clean or to kill. It was to kill. She killed the baby. My sister is unafraid again. If she had drunk the detergent to clean the baby . . . But she did not. She killed it and the sound of it being born was tlllg. And now my sister is standing. And she looks very clean. All the poison has seeped out of her too. She killed the baby but cleaned herself. She is very clean, and dry. I hope she will help me with the trash now. There is so much trash. No one has come to take the trash in the 1st and 2nd dumpsters. The dumpster truck driver is ash in my orchard. The 3rd and 4th dumpsters are filled with dirt. Dirt is dripping out of them. The dumpster area is filled with trash. It is dripping out of the 1st and 2nd dumpsters. Also the incinerator, which the landlord has ordered off. The dumpster truck driver incinerated himself. Now I have a small incinerator, but the landlord is always home. He is always home. Someone watches me through the 3rd floor stairwell window. It's hard to see. I am not sure what to do first with this small incinerator. I have to wait until the landlord leaves again on his boat. I hope my sister will help me with the trash. The roof, I think, is a good place to keep it. Until it can be burned. I have not forgotten my sister's dream of fire and of dust. I have not forgotten that dream she had. I see how clean and dry she is now. All the poison has seeped out of her. All the fluid too. Her torso is long but creaky. I am so lonely when I watch my sister bend over to laugh now. It is hard to clean when I see her long torso creaking at what is funny. Or not at what is funny but at what is befooled. Her torso is bending because she is the fool. It is like a bow. My sister has been befooled and now she is taking a bow. It was she who did the fooling and she who was fooled. It is funny twice over. Two dice. Bend over. A bow. My sister is so clean and dry and stripped now. When she bends her torso to laugh I think bow. But also bough. The bough of a pear tree. I am making an orchard and it is lonely. It is lonely. The words I have in my mouth are bough and die and dust. I think all the time now of my sister's dream of fire and of dust. What you dream should be born of what you see. Now I think it is my sister's face I have seen in the 3rd floor stairwell window. What I saw was her and what she saw was me. What you dream being born of what you see. She has seen me at the incinerator. My sister has seen me with fire and with dust. And her dream was born of that. It must have been from that. But there is a fear that always runs through me now. I see how clean my sister is now. And how dry.

And now the landlord is wearing a face mask. I had not seen him since Monday. And now it is Monday again and he is wearing a face mask. So it is the air then. It is the air that has the poison. The landlord was right. It is the air. And now he is wearing a face mask. In his own apartment. Which is the biggest. It is easiest to breathe on the 3rd floor of Slater Mill. The air is easier to breathe. And the landlord looks like a fool with his face mask. He looks like a fool but it is not funny. A mask is a mockery. The landlord is mocking us. He has a mask. What does he know. He has the bark too. All the tenants have the bark and the landlord too. Ten babies have died. It must have been the air. What does the landlord know. He is in a face mask and looks like a fool. No more babies have died because no more babies have been born. It has been strange weather. This wind. Maybe the landlord has a face mask for the wind. It keeps getting in and it brings the bark. It is too late for protection. Also, there is so much trash. I had thought it was lucky that there was a wind. There is so much trash. I had thought the wind would blow the smell away. But this wind stirs it up. The smell can never settle. The wind stirs the smell. The landlord must have a mask because of the trash. Why does he not say anything. He is the landlord. It is his loaf that smells. His big apartment. There is so much trash. The wind brings the bark and stirs the smell. He is the landlord. What does he know. Or does he not know. I think about the 2nd dream I had at Slater Mill. I do not know what it means. In that dream the blood moved in channels. And when I awoke, I wondered what the dream meant. A channel is a bed. For what is at rest and for what is dead. A bed. I thought of the river and how it had never before moved. I thought the dream must have been about the river. The morning after that dream, the river started moving again and I thought, yes, a channel is a bed. Blood in the channel. Water in the riverbed. But that was the morning that my sister was not in her bed. What does the landlord know. He knows something. He must know something. Or he knows something but does not know he knows it. It has been a long time now since my 2nd dream. Which I thought was about the river moving again. But is it about the dream or about the waking. When I awoke from my 1st dream, which was really a nightmare, I did not say the word nightmare to my sister. When I awoke from my 2nd dream, my sister was not in her bed. My 3rd dream was about my sister, and when I awoke from it, my sister told me that she had dreamt of fire and of dust. I think I must know something about my sister. But I do not know what I know. The seedlings are past time to be planted. I am barely making an orchard. My plans have been stripped down. Hold on, the maintenance man said. Did he mean stop or keep going. Orchard is still a lovely word. It is never funny. Or lonely. The landlord in his mask is funny and lonely. His mask is a mocking. There is so much trash now. And no more babies being born and no more words. No, not no more words. I am so tired. I am so tired that I said words instead of dreams. Is it the dream or the waking that is important. I am so tired. I said words instead of dreams. But maybe I knew to say that. I didn't know that I knew to say it but I said it. Dream is noise. And I said words instead of dreams. I do not know what I know.

I am barely making an orchard. That is something I am saying to myself. You are barely making your orchard. I say it because my plans have been stripped down. That is why I say barely. But that is wrong. Saturday is windows. We spray the poisons on the windows to clean them. The wind stirs up the dust and the poison. It stirs up the smell of the trash. The smell sticks to the windows. Saturday is not an easy day now. And it is wrong of me to say barely, which is not less, not not much. Barely is bare. Nakedly. Absolutely. And I am not absolutely making my orchard. And there is so much trash now on the roof and in the dumpster area. The landlord has a face mask. The wind stirs up the smell of trash. It is because of me. I was the one who made dirt in the 3rd and 4th dumpsters. I made a sign across my body with my hands. It was not the sign that I had thought it was. The dumpster truck driver and I never spoke. Empty and full were the same thing. It was good to be touched. Good and also befooling. My body was in his truck and now his body is in my orchard. I do not know if that exchange is good and true. I think it could be. But I did not know that one thing would mean the other. The dumpster truck driver came to Slater Mill with a cry. It was the cry of his brakes. He came with a cry. The driver drove his truck all day. And truck is true with the kk feeling. And anything that happens to me while I am making my orchard is good. But if it was good, why did the driver also give me his lighter. My small incinerator. It is an extra thing he gave me. Things are uneven between us now. That is, things do not quite fit. But I have an incinerator again. I have not decided

what to do with it. It's true the trash is everywhere. The tenants
see it. The landlord sees it. I have not seen the maintenance
man for some time now but I am sure he sees it. And my sister.
She sees it and more. Now I think it is my sister who watches
me from the 3rd floor stairwell window. I have been saying that
I am barely making my orchard. And I mean that I am not
really making it. But barely is naked. And I have been making
my orchard in a naked way. I have been. Everyone at Slater
Mill sees the trash. It is in the open now. The trash is there because of me. I do not know why another dumpster truck does
not arrive. I do not know why the landlord has ordered that the
incinerator stay off. Or why he has not had a new Now Leasing
flag made. I do not know who stole the flag. But everyone must
know that the trash here is because of me. I am naked now.
Everyone at Slater Mill can see Slater Orchard. They can see
it but they are dumb. I think they must be dumb. The fear runs
through me all the time now. In my channels. I awoke last night
to a loud sound. It was the bark. All the tenants have it. The
bark is so loud. But when I awoke to the sound, I thought it was
birds. I thought the bark was birds. The birds were squawk-
ing, I thought. The birds were so loud. And I thought, those
birds will wake the babies. They will wake all the babies in my
orchard ground. Which was a funny thing to think. The 3rd,
4th, 5th, 6th, 7th, 8th, and 10th babies are dead. The 1st and
2nd babies are dead somewhere else, beneath cement. The 9th
baby too is dead. It is dead and in the river. Its vocables are
in my orchard. The dumpster truck driver must have known
different words. Ard, I said. And he said, Hard. I put his ashes
in my orchard. There are cries, strange and foreign, coming

from its ground. Everything in my orchard ground is good. It is
funny that I took the bark for birds. And funny that I thought
any noise could wake the babies. Which are dead. There were
bird feathers in the maintenance man's bin. There used to be
birds at Slater Mill but they died in the cistern. They drowned
in the cistern and then the tenants started getting the mucus.
And the 8th baby was born with cysts of blue pus. There have
been no birds since then. And there have been no babies since
the 10th baby. My sister's baby was just a blue and dripping
thing. There was no body. It is funny that I took the bark for
birds and worried the noise would wake the babies. They are
dead. It is living things that want to live. I have said that dead
things want to live too. But I don't know that. I don't know that
to be true. There are cries, strange and foreign, coming from
my orchard ground. It is true that there is ground. It is new
dirt. It is true that I mean to make the dirt into an orchard. I
have not done it. Nothing is growing there. The seedlings are
still in my apartment. They are growing in tea boxes. Trees
growing inside dead trees. It is true that the dirt is not on the
cement yet. It is still inside the dumpsters. There is noise coming from the dumpster area. There is. But maybe there is not. I
hear cries. I do hear them. I do not know if dead things want to
live. There is a feeling in me that says dead things want to live.
There is a feeling that says that is true. But is the feeling itself
making the strange and foreign cries? My sister says we do not
know what is buried within our own bodies. But then she drank
the detergent. She drank the detergent and we saw what her
body had buried. And we heard it. The tlllg sound of her baby
being born. There was a sound. The cries coming from my

orchard ground . . . are strange. They could be from my body.
I had thought the cries were babies. The noise that the dust of
the babies made as the poison in their baby bodies was being
ground up. Their poison being released as cries. But the cries
could be from my body. I could be making the cries and not
know it. We don't know what is buried in our own bodies my
sister says. Except we do. We know the poison is there. And I
think there is a fear in my body too. In my channels. And now
I am thinking that it is possible the river never started moving
again. It is possible there was not a strange wind. Was the thing
moving and moving through only a fear. I am thinking that
now. It is funny to be afraid. If I am afraid, I must think something is going to happen. But nothing will. Slater made his mill
and after that nothing happened.

Mondays are the 3rd floor

Tuesdays the 2nd floor

Wednesdays ground floor

Thursdays linens

Fridays stairwells. And hallways

Saturdays windows

Sundays I do not know if I am making an orchard

The Now Leasing flag has not been flying for weeks. There is no reason for me to go out the front door of Slater Mill now. I can't remember if the flag was stolen. Or if the wind whipped it off. Or if the landlord ordered it off. Thursday is linens, but my sister and I no longer wash a flag. Even one less thing makes it easier. Though I am not sure what *it* is. Thursdays maybe. Maybe Thursdays. There is no flag for me to take down and wash and dry and fly again. There is no reason for me to go out the front door of Slater Mill now. Even one less thing makes *it* easier. Or *it* could be leaving. I am not sure what *it* is. The maintenance man has died. And now there is a whine. Even when I say, It's funny, I am not sure what *it* is. It is funny how to lease is really to leave. It is funny how loose the Now Leasing flag was when it flew. There was no wind. This strange wind came after the flag was off the pole. So it was not the wind that whipped it off. It is funny that a flag that said Now Leasing was always loose. It is funny because to lease is to loose. It is funny but I forgot for a minute that funny means someone has been befooled. Looser and looser until you can leave. The maintenance man has died. Even one less thing makes it easier. Even one less thing makes it easier is what I said to my sister on Thursday in the laundry room. We do not speak much anymore. But I did say to her, Even one less thing makes it easier. I was talking about the flag. The flag was the thing. I do not know what *it* is. But my sister let go of the sheet. She had been folding a sheet. My sister has always been very good at folding. Her body folds very easily. Her torso folds over when she laughs. Her arms fold when she smiles. Which makes it a buried smile. I am stronger than my sister. But she is very good at folding. She can double a thing over itself. When I said, Even one less thing makes it easier, my sister was folding a sheet. She let it go. She had been folding a sheet, bending it back over itself, tightly and neatly. Then her hands went loose and the sheet went loose. She let it go. But I am not sure what *it* is. The sheet of course. The maintenance man has died. It was the whine that brought me outside the front door of Slater Mill. The front door is for the tenants. It has a view of the river. It was the whine that brought me outside. That Thursday was when the whine began. But it was also my sister. My sister brought me outside. She stayed in the laundry room but something about her body brought me outside. Her body can bend back over itself. She is very good at folding. She folds all the linens. She folds over in laughter. I think she has folded over the landlord. But now she no longer lets him take her arm. She folds her arms when she smiles at me. But when I said, Even one less thing makes it easier, she went loose. The sheet went loose. Her torso was lost in the sheet. I am not sure what *it* is but I could see that my sister's body knew. Her body knew what *it* was, and I did not know. I left. It was her body that brought me outside. Also the whine. There had been a whine for a few hours. It had begun in the morning. A low whine. But its sound was taking up more space. I wanted to leave my sister's body. Her looseness made me want to leave. I pointed to my ear. The whine was taking up more space. I pointed to my ear. My sister was still loose. She nodded in a loose way and I left.

When the whine began I was in my bed. My sister was in her bed. The whine rolled through our apartment in small waves. I thought it was the seedlings. I thought, Now the seedlings are crying. They are past ready to be planted. I thought, This whine is the seedlings' cry. But the whine did not take up more space near the seedlings. I opened our apartment door. The whine rolled through the hallways in small waves. I thought, the whine is the new sound from my orchard ground. But it was not. The tenants were opening their doors too. They were following the roll of the whine. The whine rolled in small waves through the stairwells and hallways. I saw the landlord with his face mask. He was in the stairwell listening. It is the river, he said. It is the river. It was true that the whine seemed to take up more space on the river side of the mill. It is the river the landlord said through his face mask. The river is not his. The river and the air are not his, so it is easy for him to say it is the river. But the landlord was right. It was the river. We went back to our apartments. The whine was not a cry. The whine was not as bad as the bark. It was a nice break from the wind. We went back to our apartments.

I was not the 1st person to see the maintenance man. When I went out the front door of Slater Mill, there were tenants already there. It was the whine. It was taking up more space. It was rolling through the mill in bigger waves. Thursday is linens and my sister stayed in the laundry room. But some of us wanted to see the river. It was the river making the whine. The whine was rolling across the mill in such big waves. Something must be coming down the river. Or coming up out of it. The tenants went out the front door to see the river but instead they saw the maintenance man. Hold on, he had said to me in the stairwell. Hold on. He could have meant stop. Or keep going. He was a person who laid his voice flat on the ground. Though now he was in the air. Now we know where the Now Leasing flag went. The maintenance man must have taken it. It is back on the flagpole now. It is back on the flagpole with the maintenance man attached in a horrible way. He has hung himself with the Now Leasing flag. I am not sure how he did it. But he was very good at those things. He helped my sister build her cistern. He talked more to my sister than to me. People do. But he said to me, Hold on. Which is actually a perfect thing for a maintenance man to say. I don't know why I didn't see that before. Hold on is what a maintenance man is supposed to do. Stop things. And keep things going. Hold on is what a tenant does too. Hold on to the apartment. No matter what the landlord does. There is no land here. Just mills broken into partitions. Now the maintenance man has hung himself in a horrible way. It was he who stole the Now Leasing flag. I had

not seen him for some time. But there had been bird feathers
in his bin. Which was strange, because all the birds drowned in
the cistern. The tenants are upset looking at the maintenance
man. They are upset about the horrible way he has died. They
keep saying that. Which is funny. Now they are forgetting the
poison. They are forgetting the poison in the air and in the
water. The strange weather that brought the bark. Or maybe
they are not. Now they are saying, What did he know. And they
are worried about the whine. They are wondering if the whine
made the maintenance man hang himself. But the Now Leasing flag has been missing for weeks. Who is befooled here. Was
it the maintenance man. There is an order to everything. But I
cannot see it. I don't know what it is. Even one less thing makes
it easier is what I said to my sister. Now ten babies have died.
And two men. And my sister's baby, which she killed. The Now
Leasing flag hangs next to the maintenance man's body. Now
Leasing. There is an order to everything. I cannot see it. There
have been no more babies being born. And no more dreams. It
is hard to see the order without dreams and babies. Which are
the same thing. Dream is noise. Baby is babble. I am listening.
I am listening but now there is only the wind, the bark, the
whine. And the cries from the orchard ground. Which only I
can hear. Which may be coming from my body. I left the flagpole. Which is to say, I left the maintenance man. I sat in my
orchard. Which is two dumpsters full of dirt. I listened to the
cries, strange and foreign, coming from my orchard ground.
Which was a mistake. I had forgotten about my sister. I had
forgotten to think about my sister.

It is time to put the dirt on the cement. I had hoped the maintenance man would help me turn over the 3rd and 4th dumpsters. But now he has hung himself in a horrible way. Now it will take a long time. Thursday is linens but I cannot finish the linens today. I don't know what the landlord will say. But the maintenance man has died. He laid his voice low. I can see that he will need to be buried in my orchard. The only shovel is the incinerator shovel. It is the one used for ashes. My orchard is not a graveyard. It is not a graveyard! There is an order to things, though I cannot see it. The maintenance man will need to be buried. It is natural that I bury him in Slater Orchard. He was the maintenance man for Slater Mill. It is natural. Thursday is linens but I can't finish them today. The landlord might even like that I am burying the maintenance man. It is possible the landlord would have to pay for the maintenance man's burial, and funerals are dear. There is no land here. Even the landlord knows this. There is no ground for bodies to be buried in. And the landlord himself ordered the incinerator off. Though the trash is everywhere. I have been putting the trash on the roof. A lot is happening. There is a lot to think about. It would be easier if I were not trying to make an orchard. If the landlord sees the dirt, I will say it was the wind. The wind is blowing dirt and some got trapped between the dumpster area fences. Or I will say it was the river. The river is moving again and coughed up dirt. I will say, I am cleaning. I am cleaning it up. The incinerator shovel isn't as big as it should be. I have moved the 1st and 2nd dumpsters out of the dumpster area.

And I have pushed the 3rd and 4th dumpsters against the gate. No one can open the gate now. I have to climb. It would not be good for anyone but me to go into the dumpster area now. It is not a graveyard, but it is like one. On Sunday I will put the seedlings in. It is time. I have nearly all the dirt out of the 3rd dumpster and spread onto the ground. And the cries are louder. I really think they are coming from the dirt that I have made. I thought they might have been coming from my body. I was beginning to think that. But as I shovel the dirt the cries are louder. It is the dirt. It is free of the dumpster. As I shoveled I thought the cry might be the dirt. But it was my sister.

My sister is incinerating the maintenance man. The loud cries are coming from the front entrance of Slater Mill. It was my sister. She has my small incinerator. After the dumpster truck driver lit himself on fire he threw it at my feet and I had an incinerator again. But I hid it. I buried it in one of the tea boxes where my seedlings are growing. And now my sister has it. There is a lot buried between us. I buried the small incinerator. But there is a lot buried between me and my sister. Between is two each. She and I. By turns. In the space that separates me and my sister, I buried that incinerator. She took it. It is her turn. Two each. Two uses. So, four. She and I and She and I or I and I and She and She. By turns. In the space around each. I buried the incinerator. She took it. Two each. Two uses. That is between. So, fair. She took the lighter. It is her turn. She has it and she is incinerating the maintenance man. There are cries coming from the front entrance of the mill. It is my sister. She is causing the cries. They are not coming from her body. Which is silent. It is hard to know what is inside my sister. The tenants do not like that she is burning the body of the maintenance man. It is too much. He is burning just like the dumpster truck driver. Quickly. He was very dry. The wind is drying out everything. Also the whine. The whine seems to wring the water out of everything. And no one at Slater Mill drinks much water anyway. Seepage, my sister says. They boil the water for tea but the poison is still in it. The boil makes the living things in the water die. But it does not make the dead things in the water die. The boil cannot make dead things die. The parents of the dead babies tried to drink tea. They drank a lot of tea. But the poison still seeped into their babies. I do not think that fire makes the poison die either. The fire is like the boil. It kills the things that want to live. But the dead things want to live too. I don't know if the maintenance man was born alive. He went on the landlord's boat with my sister. He tried to leave. If he had left, that would be something that had happened. But he did not leave and I don't know if anything ever happened to him. Hanging. Hanging and the incinerating may be the most thing. It is hard to know what is inside my sister. Now the maintenance man and the Now Leasing flag are ash. My sister is done. She is going inside. The ash of the Now Leasing flag is part of the ash of the maintenance man. I don't know if that is good. It might be natural. I don't know. But it is funny. The maintenance man is ash now. But there is still a bit of smoke. A bit of smoke is coming from the landlord's window. He is smoking. I forgot that he must also have a small incinerator. Or more than one. It is funny how the Now Leasing flag ash and the maintenance man's ash are mixed. I am laughing. It is very funny. Something about leasing and maintaining. Leaving or holding on. I am laughing but it is hard to use words to say why. I know I am befooled. But it is hard to say why. That is the problem with being befooled. I am befooled. It is funny. I do not know what *it* is.

The trash is a problem and the landlord does not seem to see it. The trash is really a big problem. The landlord is on the phone all day but he does not seem to be talking about the trash. He does not see to be calling anyone to pick it up. He wears his face mask all the time now. Even when he smokes. He has to smoke at an odd angle. Maybe the smell of the smoking is a mask for the smell of the trash. The smell is a problem but also the trash itself. The roof is almost full. I have filled just about every open area on the roof with trash. There is nowhere else for it to go. The tenants have noticed. When I empty the bins, the trash just goes to another part of the mill. The roof. The trash cannot leave. We have a trash roof. It is funny. I am laughing all the time now. Rough is how we say roof. A rough of trash. Rough also sounds like a gentle bark. Though the tenants' bark is dying down. And the wind is dying down. Which makes the whine easier to hear. I bring each bin of trash up to the roof. My legs hurt. I am always going up the stairs with bins. I don't understand why the landlord does not see it. The tenants are saying to put the trash in the river. The river is moving again they say. It makes sense to put the trash in the river. There are not many more days before the roof is full. But a roof of trash is perfect and funny. A roof of trash is perfect and perfect is the end. A roof of trash is very funny. This is the only way I am not dumb. My mouth is open. My eyes are open. I am not the fool. A rough of trash. It is perfect and the end. Put the trash in the river. That's what the tenants are saying. But I have to think about the sea. The river is dead but there is still a sea. I think there is a sea. Though it could be a sea full of trash. Which would be perfect too. A seaful of trash and a skyful of trash. Then it would be perfect. I am laughing all the time now. Even though my legs hurt. The only times I am not laughing are when I am with my sister or when I am playing with the bird bones that the maintenance man left or when I am making my orchard.

Maybe it's because the tenants no longer have the bark that the whine is taking up more space. The wind is gone, and the whine is rolling in bigger waves down the river. There is a feeling that something is coming. A heat maybe. It feels like a heat is coming. I am always going up the stairs with bins. The roof is really full of trash. The trash rolls in waves across the roof. I am standing on the roof and the trash is washing toward me in waves. If I had a boat. If I had a boat up on this roof, I could go up and down on the waves of trash. That is how it feels. But it is not good. The fear runs through me in waves. There is a feeling that something is coming. The whine is taking up more space. The roof is full of trash. I empty the bins but on the roof. The windows on the third floor are cracking. It could be the whine. It is taking up more space. Or it could be the trash. The roof is so heavy with trash. I don't know why the landlord doesn't see it. When I cleaned out the maintenance man's apartment, the toys were there. Toys made from the bones of birds. The bones were very clean. He must have bleached them.

If I had a boat I would ride in the waves of trash. That is how it feels. But I would not go anywhere. There is nowhere to go. Trash is fallen leaves. That is one of the first words I looked up in my dictionary. It is funny that trash is the word I looked up. My dictionary is burned but I can still look up trash. It is all over the roof. Trash is fallen leaves. The tenants are trees and their leaves fall from them into the bins. The tea boxes and tea bags fall into the bins. The landlord's fruit cores. The maintenance man's bird feathers fell into his bin. Though he was not a bird. Though he did hang himself in the sky. The bones of his birds were very clean. They must have been bleached. I am laughing all the time now. Unless I am playing with these bone toys. Though playing may not be the right word. I am holding them. Holding the bone toys. Hold on, the maintenance man said in the stairwell. I have the bones in my hands. The fear runs through me in waves. It weaves. The fear is making something. Slater is a mill after all. Slater milled denim. I am making an orchard. And the fear is making something. It runs through me in waves. It is weaving something in me. I don't think it is the end. I think the end is already made. I don't know if it is funny that the fear is weaving something in me. It is either funny or perfect. I am either a fool or an end.

The mill is condemned. Slater Mill has been condemned. That must be why the landlord wears a face mask. He must think he knows something that the tenants do not know. He must think he knows something about a poison that the tenants do not know. That must be why the landlord does not see the trash, which is everywhere. It is really a problem. And no new dumpster truck driver comes. This must be why. Slater Mill is condemned. Still, the landlord does not leave. If I had a boat, I would ride up and down the waves of trash. To think of the trash as a sea, something with sides, something to be crossed, makes it easier. I do not know what *it* is. The mill is condemned. And the whine has brought a foam. And the landlord and the tenants stay. The landlord must stay for money. And the tenants must stay because they must stay. Tenants hold on. And my seedlings are in the ground now. There are 16 seedlings in my orchard ground. I count all the time. 16 must stay at Slater Mill. Tenants hold on. If a word is the truth, the tenants must stay. I did not know if the dream I had of 16 pear trees in Slater Orchard was a true thing. A dream is noise. The noise of words gone soft. The noise of what is true taking up more space. I think I am losing my precision. There is so much that has happened. I am tired. It would be easier if I were not making an orchard. I dreamt of 16 pear trees. I thought then that 16 trees made for a bare orchard. It would not take long to walk through an orchard of 16 trees. Now I think 16 is a large number. Ten babies have died. My sister's baby did not really have a body but it also died. The maintenance man died. The dumpster truck driver. Now

I count all the time. This mill is condemned. I am very tired. If this mill is condemned then does that mean this making is condemned. I am making an orchard. The mill is condemned. Making is condemned. Slater Mill and Slater Orchard will end in fire.

It was my sister who saw the landlord hang the condemned sign. She walks the building often now. She says the whine wakes her at night. The whine sounds like a baby's cry, she says. But it is not a cry. The whine is not sharp like a cry. It is dull. It is dull and it rolls out in waves. My sister wakes and walks the building. On the river side, the whine is very clear. It cracks the windows and it sounds even clearer near the cracks. My sister walks the building. She walks every floor except the roof. And she has such a long torso. She is always bending it. And she is so dry now, so dry that she creaks. She is always bending and creaking. Now there is no difference between her laughing and her crying. The whine wakes her at night and she walks. She is looking for a baby. She is looking for a baby, but she does not go to the orchard ground. So it is not a dead baby that she is looking for. And I don't think the cries from the orchard ground are the cries she hears. It is the whine she hears. She was looking for a baby, she said, and she saw the landlord. He had on his face mask. He had a piece of paper in one hand and a piece of tape in the other. He was hanging a sign. This was on the 1st floor hallway. The parents of the 4th baby to die live in that hallway. Theirs is the door closest to the entrance. Or exit. The landlord was hanging a sign. It was the middle of the night. Did he have on his mask, I asked my sister. She bent and said, His face is a mockery. He was hanging a sign that said the property was condemned. It hung very close to the door of the parents of the 4th baby to die. Was that the baby who died with vocables in its fist. Or was that the baby whose testicles looked like an orchid. There is too much. But it is important to count. 16 will stay. What did you do, I asked my sister. What did you do when you saw him. My sister no longer needs to smile at me. Her torso moves and bends. Over and under. It is the woof. I do not know what the warp is. What did you do when you saw him. She does not say anything. My sister is good at disappearing. She is good and quiet. Sometimes I think she is gone. But she does have a body. She does have a body. Even if she can quiet its creaking, she has a body. And I think she can do that. I think she can quiet her own creaking. If she needed to. My sister and I are both good at being quiet. We have always picked quiet over confrontation. We are very good at hiding our faces. I do not need a face mask and neither does my sister. But we have bodies. My sister is good and quiet but she has a body. What did you do when you saw him. It was a silly question. And it was not. My sister was walking in the middle of the night. She was looking for a baby. She said, Then I saw the landlord. She said, he was in a face mask and he was hanging a sign that said Slater Mill has been condemned. All that she was saying was funny. I am laughing all the time now. But I do not laugh in front of my sister. Laughing makes more laughter and I do not want my sister to laugh like I am laughing. She is very dry. When she bends, she creaks. Her torso is the woof. Her body is making something. If she laughed like I laugh, her bones would break. What did you do when you saw him. Nothing, she said. Nothing. Nothing of course. But nothing is not nothing. Nothing looks like nothing. But nothing is waiting. Nothing is waiting for a man to stop doing what he is doing. Nothing is waiting out a man. Nothing is waiting for the

man to be over. And then doing something. Nothing is hiding
your face.

I walked to the river edge with the tenants. The tenants are at the river edge all the time now. The whine has brought a blue foam. It is hard to describe. My sister stayed inside to clean and I could not describe it to her. The whine is boiling the river. And now there is the blue foam. The tenants are afraid to touch it. But the foam wants to be touched. It is bright blue. It looks very delicate. It is definitely poison. Only poison could be so bright. It is brighter blue than any denim dye. The tenants are afraid to touch it. I think the foam looks delicate. Comely is the word. It wants to be touched. Come closer, the foam is saying. Slater Mill is condemned. I think it must end in fire. And the tenants must stay because they must. And 16 will be in the orchard. Will be of the orchard. It is not a graveyard. In my mind, 13 are there already. Even though the 1st and 2nd babies to die are not in the orchard. Their parents had to pay for their burials. Their bodies are someplace else. But they are part of my orchard ground. I remember my sister saying what a shame the parents had to pay for a dead baby's burial. I remember my sister building a cistern. She thought she could make the water clean. She thought she could stop the seepage. It began with the 1st and 2nd babies and so they are part of my orchard ground. That is the way seepage works.

I am counting all the time now. I count an orchard of 13. I count 3 more to go. I think the end is already made. I want to keep the nightmare contained. I am counting. I do not know if my sister and I were born alive but after we were born nothing happened. The sea will not happen. Poison has happened. I think the end is already made but then there is the fear. Which is also making something in me. In waves. The fear is weaving. And my sister's body is weaving. My sister walks the hallways at night. It is the whine that wakes her. The whine is bringing the river to a boil. But it is babble my sister hears. She thinks she hears a baby. I don't think there could be a baby at Slater Mill. Slater Mill has slayed all the babies. The landlord says it is the air. It is the air and it is also the water. It is the river. The dye killed it. Now it is killing the tenants. The dye or the river. What it is I don't know. I am so busy counting and laughing. And cleaning. When I clean I laugh because the poison is everywhere. My sister and I are only moving it around. Although the flies really are a problem. The dead flies do need to be cleaned up. It is the trash. I count only a few more days until the roof is holding all the trash it can. No new dumpster truck driver is coming. The property is condemned. The landlord's loaf smells very, very bad. Still, he is staying. There is his boat. It must be the move-out fee. My sister says that the landlord must be staying to collect the move-out fee. All tenants have one week to move out. Or else there is a fee. My sister said that. Or she heard that. The landlord is very true to landlord. He is true to his word. He must be hoping that the tenants are true to their word. He must be hoping that the tenants are true tenants. If they stay, he will collect a fee. My sister and I have not talked about what will happen when the week is up. We are cleaning as usual. And really nothing has happened. The mills go on for miles. Nothing has happened. But *nothing* is waiting for the man to be over. My sister hears a baby crying. She still has the small incinerator. And I have a fear weaving within me. My sister's body is weaving something too.

The dead flies need to be cleaned up. We have tried sweeping them, but they are too sticky. The fly bodies stick to the floor and to the windowsills. The bristles of the broom do nothing but open up the fly bodies. Then a blood that looks like pus comes out. Brooms do not work. Opening up is a kind of cleaning. The blue dictionary was the first thing I burned. I do not know what to clean really is. But the word clean in my mouth is an opening. My mouth opens in a precise way to say clean. My mouth opens down for clean. Close it or the flies will come in. They are everywhere. It is the trash. We spray them with the cleaning spray. Which kills. Then the bristles of the broom break the flies open. I don't know if my sister and I will keep cleaning when the week is over. If we keep cleaning, maybe we will not have to pay the move-out fee. I do not think I can move out. I have Slater Orchard to think about. It does not look like an orchard yet. If someone could get into the dumpster area, the seedlings would get stepped on. A driver in a truck would not even see the seedlings. A body walking fast through the dumpster area would definitely step on a seedling. The seedlings are not tall yet. They are up to my ankle. They need water twice a day. It is all the ash. The ash in the orchard ground is so thirsty for water. Dead things want to live. I have to water the seedlings twice a day. The dirt is always very dry. The ash is greedy for water. The fruit will definitely be poisoned fruit. I cannot help the poison in the water. And in the air. Though the orchard ground is grinding away. The strange cries are loud. It could be the cries of the bodies. It could be. It would make sense that the cries were the cries of the babies. Dead things want to live. I want to live very much. I want to live and I want my sister to live. She is younger than I am. She has a torso like a riverbend. I don't know if my sister and I were born alive but I want to live very much. My sister would be good at living. She would be very good at making things happen. It is true that the poison is in her. But poison is a drink. And my sister's body is very dry. She bled the poison out of her body with her baby. She bled it and the baby out. Everything was blue. It seeped out of her. It took days. Now she is dry and creaking. It's true that she is drinking water and she is breathing air. So the poison is seeping back into her. But I think the poison must work slowly. My sister could have something happen. She could have a 2nd baby. She could go to the sea. If there is a sea at the end of the river, my sister could go to it. A sea might be able to swallow all the poison. It is possible. It may not be good to say that my sister's torso is like a riverbend. I may only say that because a riverbend is the only natural thing here that I can see. Her torso is not like an apartment or a stairwell or a window or a flagpole or a bottle of cleaning spray. I worry that I have condemned my sister. I said her torso was like a riverbend. I do not want to be true to my words. I should have said that my sister's torso was like the sea. I want my sister to live. If she bent over the river into this blue foam . . . I do not want riverbend to be the end of my sister. The landlord said the mill is condemned. Which means fire. A fire is coming and my sister has a small incinerator. And I have said charred so many times. I have kept charred in my mouth for a very long time. The word orchard has been in my mouth. It has been like a pearl in my mouth. But now the word sounds to me like just a possibility. We might be drowned in the river. Or, charred. I have said it so many times. The strange and foreign cries coming from my orchard ground are loud. It could be the bodies. But they are already dust. Except for the 10th baby, who is bones now. The bodies are mostly dust but the dirt is still grinding. I think it is the poison. I think the cry is the cry of poison being killed. The poison was already particulate. It was already very small. There must be a terrible process to grind up particulates. They are already so small. To cut in half a grain and to cut the halves in half. It must be a terrible process. The poison was already particulate. Now the orchard ground is cutting it up. Now poison is spoon and sip and sop. The orchard ground is snipping the poison particulates into no and in and is. It must be a terrible process. To cut a thing into so many pieces. To cut until *it* is no longer itself.

Thursday. Linens. My sister and I have slipped notes under the tenants' doors. We will wash their linens too. If they are leaving or if they are staying. The property is condemned. There will be a fire soon. And a move-out fee for those who stay. The flies are everywhere. It is the smell of the trash on the roof. But there is not enough trash for all the flies. They want any kind of stain or spill. The flies have started living on the tenants. It is hard to wash clothes in the sinks here. The tenants' sinks are small and do not drain well. The landlord would not like it if we were using his machines and his water to wash the tenants' clothes. Even if his water is poison. Even if it leaves a blue tinge. The well the water comes from is the landlord's. He is lord of the water. The tenants have already started bringing their linens. They are bringing them in handfuls. They are quiet. My sister nods to them and pins a slip of paper to each handful. The slip of paper is the apartment number. Friday when we are cleaning the hallways we will leave the handfuls of linens at each apartment. It is funny we have never washed the tenants' clothes before. It is funny the landlord made us so afraid. There is no land here. The mills go on for miles. He is a little man who talks on the phone. He is always on the phone. He talks and smokes. He is really a very little man. It is funny we were too afraid to use the landlord's water and the landlord's machine for the tenants. I am glad for the cistern my sister and the maintenance man built. I am glad for Slater Orchard. I am making it but I do not want to be lord of it. I want to make it. To knead it but not keep it. My sister is nodding to the tenants as they bring their handfuls. She is bending and nodding. She is a woof. Her warp is all goodness. The fear is in me. Something is waiting. But what my sister is making is all good. What the fear is making in me is a sharpness. It jabs. Maybe it is the blue foam that is making the fear in me. The foam wants to be touched. It is bright, bright blue. It looks delicate. Bright delicate foam. Anything so bright must be bad. It must be a very bad poison. The whine has been with us for weeks now. It is the river boiling. I can feel the heat from the river while on the roof. The heat makes the smell of the trash even worse. But the foam has a delicate smell. It might be lavender. Real lavender. The foam smells like a plant or like a flower. It does not smell like poison. My sister went out to the river edge. She had not seen the foam before. The tenants are always outside now. The smell of the trash is a little better outside. And the blue foam is getting brighter. Though the whine is hard to bear. The river is at a boil and the whine cannot be borne. But then there is the foam. Such a bright blue and so delicate. It wants to be touched. The tenants watch the foam. It is rising. They watch it but they are not fools. They are not fools. The foam wants to be touched but the tenants would not touch it. They could not have foreseen the wave. The river is moving again, yes, but it has stayed in its bed. The nightmare is contained. It is just that the foam is very good to look at. And it has a delicate smell. But the tenants were not fooled by the delicacy. It is just that the delicate smell is a relief. And relief is lightness. Anything can be borne with a lightness like that. Relief is a lightness and the foam was very bright. The riverbend was not lonely at all. Also the air was lighter. The river was moving again but all its poison was in the foam. So the poison was rising, yes, but not into the air. Or not as much. The nightmare was contained. A relief. A rising. A lightness. And my sister had gone outside to see the foam. She was bending and nodding. She was a woof and her warp was all goodness. It was really a very good Thursday. Good maybe because it was the last at Slater Mill. Or the last one on the lease. Good because of the foam. Which felt so good to see. And very good because my sister and I were using the landlord's water and the landlord's machines to wash the tenants' clothes. No one could have foreseen the wave. And the wave is not something that happened. A wave came, yes, but nothing happened. Slater built his mill and after that nothing happened. A wave came. It was the boiling. The boil made a wave in the water. My sister said the whine got louder and then there was the wave. A wave of blue foam. The delicate smell of a real plant was strong. Lavender maybe. But the wave splashed some of the tenants. It was poison after all. The wave splashed some of the tenants and burned them. They died. The wave burned them weirdly. It was a water that did not wet. It dried. They died. It burned them weirdly. They were not meant to be so close to the river. But my sister said to me, Where else were they meant to be. The wave burned them weirdly. The river bent and turned. It left its bed. Dead things want to live of course. Many of the tenants died. As soon as the foam touched them they dried up and died. Where else were they meant to be said my sister. She did not die. She was not close enough to the river edge. And when the wave went back into the river, my sister stepped back. She did not step forward to see. Which was good. It was good you did not step forward, I said to her later. And she looked at me. Another wave came. Another wave of foam. It

took the tenants' bodies. Which was for the best. I said that to
my sister too. When she told me the second wave took the tenants' bodies I said, It is for the best. And she looked at me. Best,
she said. We continued folding the linens. It was the flies I had
been thinking of. They are everywhere. They are already living
on any stain or spill. If they were also eating and drinking from
the burned bodies . . . Though the whine has stopped. Which
really is good. The river must have finally reached its boil. The
foam is rolling. The whine is gone. Now there are the waves.

Friday. More of the tenants have died. My sister and I think
more may have died. We tried to deliver the clean linens on Friday. We had handfuls of linens to give back to the tenants. But
so many apartments were empty. Empty in a strange way. Tea-
pots boiling dry on the stove but no one home. My sister and
I counted how many tenants died in the 1st wave. We counted
how many strangely empty apartments. It could be that the
tenants have moved out. The lease is over after all. We are all
counting days. Though we may not all leave. One mill may
be the same as the other. My sister and I are counting tenants
now too. It is the foam. It wants to be touched. And the whine
is gone. It does seem good to stand at the river edge and smell
the foam. It seems good. But the waves burn and dry. Skin
and hair. Skin and hair only. The foam does not seem to eat
the landlord's boat. The foam does not eat the rocks along the
river. It is only skin and hair that it seems to burn. And where
is the landlord. My sister says that when she tried to deliver his
linens, his door was locked. My sister and I have pushed two of

the dumpsters to the front of the mill. We are trying to block
the entrance. Or exit. We do not want tenants to see the foam.
It is possible that some tenants do not yet know that the river
can leave its bed. It is best to see the foam from the windows.
It really is comely. Come closer the foam says. And it smells
like pears. Its smell is very good. But a smell is a smolder. This
foam smells good but it is a smolder. The waves of foam burn
and dry. The landlord has said nothing. The waves burn and
dry. Or is it the smell of the waves that burns. I know the mill
will end in fire. The trash smell or the wave smell. A smell is a
smolder. Maybe Slater Mill will end this way. We blocked the
front entrance with dumpsters. The tenants are blocked in. But
many cannot walk out to the river easily anyway. They have
the creak. Now that the whine has stopped we can all hear the
creak. When some of the tenants walk there is a sound. It is
their bones. They have the creak. They must walk slowly. That
is good in a way. Now it will take too long for them to walk
to the river edge. I don't know if my sister has the creak. Her
bones only make a sound when she bends. When she walks it
is fine. And I don't know why she is walking with a scissor. She
is smiling. She says that she does not need the scissor anymore.
She says that I can have the scissor to dig a trench. This is
the last week of the lease and there is so much to do for my
orchard. Even if the landlord does not make us clean anymore
I will be very busy with the orchard. The ash in my orchard
ground is always parched. If the landlord turns off the water I
will need to dig a trench from the river to my orchard. It will be
hard. There is so much cement. And now there are the waves
to worry about. And if I get the creak I may not be strong

enough to slice the cement. It's the bones. They get weak and dry and they creak. If I have to dig a trench I don't know what to do about the foam. It is such strong poison. Will my orchard ground be able to break it. The ground has 10 babies. Their bodies or not their bodies, 10 babies have seeped into it. Plus my sister's baby. Which was a leak. There are 2 men and vocables and a dictionary. These things could be equal to poison. Or be more than poison. These things are what is true. They may equal more than poison. I am counting all the time. I am counting all the time but not the days since my sister has slept. I had thought it was the whine waking her at night. The whine woke her and she walked. But the whine has stopped. The river has reached its boil. Still my sister wakes. She says there is a baby crying.

Sunday. The last Sunday on the lease. The seedlings are growing quickly. Most of the seedlings are growing quickly. They
love the ash. But ash is parched. I will need to water my orchard ground all the time. And when the lease is up I don't
know about the well. Will the well be turned off. I may have to
make another cistern. Or a trench. A trench from my orchard
to the river. I don't know what the landlord will do if he sees
a trench. Though the property is condemned. It is ending in
fire. But until it ends, it is his. Though I have not seen him.
When my sister went to deliver his linens his door was locked.
My sister and I are counting tenants. We think more may have
died in other waves. I am also counting orchard trees. 13 of the
seedlings are growing quickly. 3 of the seedlings are not. They
seem to be waiting to grow. Their stalks are thin, very thin. I
have to be careful when I water them that the water does not
bend their stalks. Today is an important Sunday. Last one on
the lease. I am putting the bird bones into the orchard today. I
really should have put the bird bones in a long time ago. Even
a stripped-down orchard needs birds. The maintenance man
must have known that. He was always up on the roof making repairs. He was up high often. I think it was maybe the
maintenance man whose face I saw in the 3rd floor stairwell
window. It was his face in that dirty window. I have not seen a
face in that window for a long time now. So maybe it was the
maintenance man's. Though I have not seen the landlord in a
long time either. My sister said that his door was locked. He
hung the condemned sign and since then no one has seen him.

My sister saw him hang the sign. She watched him hang the sign and she did nothing. Which is a kind of waiting. When I cleaned out the maintenance man's apartment I found toys. Bird bones made into toys. The bone toys are very bright. The maintenance man must have bleached them. The bone toys are good to hold. They are smooth and clean. I don't know what the maintenance man meant when he said Hold on. Stop. Or keep going. Or maybe grip. Grip. If he meant grip it would be my sister's hand. It would be my sister's hand I would grip.

Monday. 3rd floor. Landlord's door. I came to empty his bins. Which is funny. Who is befooled. It is the landlord. There is nowhere for the trash. The roof is full. The smell from the trash is terrible. The property is condemned. It will end in fire. And now my sister has given me a scissor. She gave me a scissor to make a trench for my orchard ground. It is a large scissor. And sharp. But it is alone. One long jab. It is not a pair of scissors. It cannot cut. Only jab. It was nice of my sister to share the scissor with me. I have a scissor and I think my sister has a scissor. I think I saw her scissor in her apron pocket. When the lease is up I will dig a trench for my orchard. I will jab the cement and make a trench. I am not better than my sister. She is better than I. She is all goodness. Though the fear is making something in me. It is making something inside me. And my sister is making something. She bends. She is the woof. What is the warp. Something is turning. It is not the knob on the landlord's door. Which is locked. I cannot count the days since I last saw him. My sister saw him hang the condemned sign. After that, nothing happened. I cannot empty his bins and my sister cannot dust his apartment. I know that the ending is fire. I think the end is already made. But the fear is making something else. And I am making an orchard. It is hard to make all good things. All goodness. It is very hard. My sister has a small incinerator and maybe a scissor. But she is better than I. When I turn to tell her that the landlord's door is still locked, she smiles. We go to the next apartment. We have decided that I should empty the bins into the laundry room today. There are no more Thursdays on the lease. No more linens. And the roof is full. There is not much trash on the 3rd floor today. It is quiet and clean on the 3rd floor. Quiet and clean. Quiet is a rest. A rest in a bed. And clean is an opening. And the landlord's door is locked. But it is his door to lock. Don't look into things. Don't look up. Don't look through the lock.

The baby cannot be an alive baby. It is crying. But that doesn't have to mean it is alive. I have heard it now too. It is the baby whose cry my sister hears at night. It was not the whine. It was this 2nd floor baby. My sister and I heard a cry as we cleaned. It was a baby. It could not be an alive baby. The cry was the same one as the night cry. That is what my sister said. We heard a cry and my sister said that it was a cry she knew from at night. The dead baby is calling to us she said. It was calling at night and now it is calling during the day. The dead baby was calling from the 2nd floor. I brought a bin to the laundry room and emptied it. I could not hear the cry. I brought the bin back to the 2nd floor and there was the cry again. My sister said, It is calling from this floor. We heard it through a door. It was loudest through one door but that door was locked. My sister took her scissor. It is true then that we both have a scissor. She took hers and jabbed it into the lock. My sister is stronger than I thought. The baby could not be an alive baby but it was. It was an alive baby. It was only a little bit blue. This was the last Tuesday on the lease. The baby was only a little bit blue. It was the 11th baby. And 11 is one left. Only a little bit blue and a girl. It was crying. There were no parents. So many tenants had run outside to see the foam. No parents. It could have been the wave. My sister jabbed her scissor into the lock on the tenants' door. And there was the 11th baby. Alive. 11 is one left. I wanted this baby to leave. It was only a little bit blue. 11 is one leaves. We will wait through the last Tuesday on the lease and the last Wednesday on the lease. And if there are no parents, we will put the baby on the landlord's boat.

I want to know what everything means and I cannot know. When we saw the 11th baby my sister bent down and picked it up. She bent and creaked. She held the baby and bent and creaked. It was then I thought that Slater was the word that was wrong. Slater was the word that went wrong. A slater is a roofmaker. Someone who makes roofs out of rock. But the rock breaks easily. A slater is a splinter worker. His rock breaks. His rock is good for roofs but I think it is the wrong kind of rock. I think it is the wrong rock. My sister bends and creaks. She is rocking the alive baby. Her torso rocks. Rock the baby. Slater is the wrong kind of rock. I do not know if the rock for roofs and the rock for babies was ever the same word. The blue dictionary is burned. But it is easy to imagine rock being the same thing once. A man is bending and creaking to pluck a rock from the ground. Rock is something plucked. And rock is the motion made when plucking the thing from the ground. Bend and pluck and bend and pluck. The thing in the ground is called rock. And the motion of taking the thing from the ground is called rock. It is easy for me to make Slater's rock and my sister's rock into the same thing. A motion. It is the motion that is important and not the thing. My sister bent and plucked the baby. She bent and creaked. Hers is a motion to pick up babies and pears. It is a motion one makes when plucking pears that have fallen to an orchard ground. Back and forth and up and down. That is my sister's rock. It is easy for me to imagine that Slater's rock and my sister's rock are really the same word. If rock and rock were the same what would that mean.

It would be easy to say that there is where *it* went wrong. Rock should have meant bending and creaking with a baby. Bending to pluck the pears. They were the same word once and then things went wrong. The slater splintered the rock. And one Slater got rich and made a mill and nothing happened. If the rock were not splintered . . . This would all be nice to say. It would be nice but I don't know if it is true.

Thursday. It is funny. The lease is over. We are off the lease. But still Thursday has linens. We wrapped the baby in clean linens. Though there is no such thing as clean. Poison is everywhere. We wrapped the baby in linens cleaned with pure poison. The lease had ended and no one has seen the landlord. When we saw the 11th baby my sister and I had the same plan. Wrap the baby in linens and send it to the sea. We will put the baby on the landlord's boat and send it to the sea. A sea. If there is one. If there is one left. I would have liked my sister to leave. She will not. She is making something. She has a scissor and a small incinerator. She is all goodness. But there is a fear in me. As soon as my sister and I saw the alive baby we had the same plan. Send the baby to the sea. 11 is one left. One who leaves. The lease is up. Leave. It is I who need to be left. And my sister who needs to leave. Slater Mill will end in fire. The landlord's paper said condemned. I don't know how the fire will start. It is maybe already started. Maybe the smell of the trash is hiding the smolder. Maybe the foam is the fire. When my sister is asleep I will take her scissor. I will take back the small incinerator. My sister is all goodness. It is I who is demoness of corpses.

The toys made of bird bones are going in the center of my orchard. The toys are for the dead babies. And bones make a very good dust. And the trees of an orchard need birds. To peck at the pears. Really, birds can be a nuisance. And a nuisance is not nothing. A nuisance is really death. It's a death that we pretend is not important. Not very important. It is good to call things a nuisance. It is natural. It would be good to have an orchard of 16 pear trees and to have birds pecking at the fruit. It would be good to have a nuisance. To say, Oh, this death is not important. Oh, the birds are pecking at the pears again! That is something I would like to say. I would like to say it to my sister and to have her laugh. My sister would bend as she laughed and her warp and her woof would be making linen jackets for the pears. Her laughing and bending would be part of her weaving jackets for each pear. To stop the birds from pecking. Yes, the bird bones should be buried in the center of the orchard. Bones are a very good beginning. There is an order to everything. Bones are first. I am making Slater Orchard. The bird bones will make the flesh of the pears bone white. The flesh of the pears will not be poison blue. They will be bone white. My sister will keep a pear in her apron pocket. And when she is laughing the pear will roll out of her pocket. And she will bend her long torso and pick it up. And these flies. They will turn to fireflies. My sister will hold up the small incinerator. She will light a fly body. The wings keep beating. The wings beat the burning body. She lights another. We count how long each flame lasts. It does not last long. My sister holds the small incinerator and lights fly body after fly body. The wings beat the burning bodies. It is a good way to get rid of flies. Which are a nuisance. Which is a death we say is unimportant. The fire grinds the particulates of the fly bodies. The fire grinds them and changes them. The next flies to be born are fireflies. And my sister and I sit. It is night in the orchard. We are sharing a pear between us. We are sitting on the orchard ground. Which is good. There is even moss. Maybe the pear is sweet. Very sweet. It is orchard night. The fireflies are fire. Then ash. Then fire. Then ash.

I was daydreaming. I was daydreaming of my sister holding a small incinerator. Which is silly. She is all goodness. She would not light a fly body on fire. Though the flies are everywhere. It was not an incinerator. My sister is holding a scissor. When I water the orchard I do daydream. It is probably the poison. I do daydream but it is probably just the poison. Seepage. I am laughing. I am laughing and counting all the time. 13 seedlings doing well. 3 seedlings very thin. I count my sister and me and the landlord left. The fear is making a sum in me. A sum is the highest. The highest reckoning. I dreamt of 16 pear trees in my orchard ground. There is a sum here that I do not want to say. My sister had a dream of fire and of dust. I dreamt of an orchard with 16 pear trees. I do not want to say whose dream was right. Which dream was good. And I cannot say now what is real and what is dream. Or really I cannot tell now what I have dreamt into happening from what I have done after dreaming. My sister is all goodness. What she makes will be right and good. The fear in me is making a sum. The highest reckoning. Do not look up. Look down at the orchard ground. The fear is making a sum in me. But I will stop counting. It is not the reckoning I want to fill my mouth. It is a pear. I would like to eat a pear. It is funny how I do not have a pear. I do not have a pear to put there. And pear is too bare a word. But orchard. Here is the word orchard in my mouth. Or charred. A good tree will bring forth good fruit.